OF ALL THINGS!

OF ALL THINGS!

BY

ROBERT C. BENCHLEY

A COMMON READER EDITION
THE AKADINE PRESS

These sketches appeared originally in *Vanity Fair, The New York Tribune Sunday Magazine, Collier's Weekly, Life,* and *Motor Print,* all but two of these magazines immediately afterward having either discontinued publication or changed hands. To those which are old enough to remember, and to the new managements of the others, the author offers grateful acknowledgment for permission to reprint the material in this book. (As a matter of fact, permission was never asked, but they probably won't mind anyway.)

PREFACE

WHEN, in the Course of human events, it becomes necessary for one people to dissolve the political bands which have connected them with another, and to assume among the powers of the earth, the separate and equal station to which the Laws of Nature and of Nature's God entitle them, a decent respect to the opinions of mankind requires that they should declare the causes which impel them to the separation.

We hold these truths to be self-evident,—that all men are created equal, that they are endowed by their Creator with certain unalienable Rights; that among these are Life, Liberty and the pursuit of Happiness. That to secure these rights, Governments are instituted among Men, deriving their just powers from the consent of the governed,—That whenever any Form of Government becomes destructive of these ends, it is the Right of the People to alter or to abolish it, and to institute new Government, laying its foundation on such principles and organizing its powers in such form, as to them shall seem most likely to effect their Safety and Happiness. Prudence, indeed, will dictate that Governments long established should not be changed for light and transient causes; and accordingly all experience hath shewn, that mankind are more disposed to suffer, while evils are sufferable, than to right themselves by abolishing the forms to which they are accustomed. But when a long train of abuses and usurpations, pursuing invariably the same Object, evinces a design to reduce them under absolute Despotism, it is their right, it is their duty, to throw off such Government, and to provide new Guards for their own future security. Such has been the patient sufferance of these Colonies; and such is now the necessity which constrains them to alter their former Systems of Government. The history of the present King of Great Britain is a history of repeated injuries and usurpations, all having in direct object the establishment of an absolute Tyranny over these States. To prove this, let Facts be submitted to a candid world.

R. C. B.

"The Rookery"
Breeming Downs
Wippet-cum-Twyne
New York City
August 24, 1921

CONTENTS

ix

CONTENTS

TABLOID EDITIONS

OF ALL THINGS!

I

THE SOCIAL LIFE OF THE NEWT

I T is not generally known that the newt, although one of the smallest of our North American animals, has an extremely happy home-life. It is just one of those facts which never get bruited about.

"Since that time I have practically lived among the newts."

I first became interested in the social phenomena of newt life early in the spring of 1913, shortly after I had finished my researches in sexual differentiation among ameba. Since that time I have practically lived among newts, jotting down observations, making lantern-slides, watching them in their work and in their play (and you may rest assured that the little rogues have their play—as who does not?) until, from much lying in a research posture on my stomach, over the inclosure in which they were confined, I found myself developing what I

[3]

feared might be rudimentary creepers. And so, late this autumn, I stood erect and walked into my house, where I immediately set about the compilation of the notes I had made.

So much for the non-technical introduction. The remainder of this article bids fair to be fairly scientific.

In studying the more intimate phases of newt life, one is chiefly impressed with the methods by means of which the males force their attentions upon the females, with matrimony as an object. For the newt is, after all, only a newt, and has his weaknesses just as any of the rest of us. And I, for one, would not have it different. There is little enough fun in the world as it is.

The peculiar thing about a newt's courtship is its restraint. It is carried on, at all times, with a minimum distance of fifty paces (newt measure) between the male and the female. Some of the bolder males may now and then attempt to overstep the bounds of good sportsmanship and crowd in to forty-five paces, but such tactics are frowned upon by the Rules Committee. To the eye of an uninitiated observer, the pair might be dancing a few of the more open figures of the minuet.

The means employed by the males to draw the attention and win the affection of those of the opposite sex (females) are varied and extremely strategic. Until the valuable researches by Strudlehoff in 1887 (in his "*Entwickelungsmechanik*") no one had been able to ascertain just what it was that the male newt did to make the female see anything in him worth throwing herself away on. It had been observed that the most personally unattractive newt could advance to within fifty paces of a female of his acquaintance and, by some *coup d'œil*, bring her to a point where she would, in no uncertain terms, indicate her willingness to go through with the marriage ceremony at an early date.

It was Strudlehoff who discovered, after watching several thousand courting newts under a magnifying lens (questionable taste on his part, without doubt, but all is fair in pathological love) that the male, during the courting season (the season opens on the tenth of March and extends through the following February, leaving about ten days for general overhauling and redecorating) gives forth a strange, phosphorescent glow from the center of his highly colored dorsal crest, somewhat similar in effect to the flash of a diamond scarf-pin in a red necktie. This glow, according to Strudlehoff, so fascinates the female with its air of elegance and indication of wealth, that she immediately falls a victim to its lure.

[5]

But the little creature, true to her sex-instinct, does not at once give evidence that her morale has been shattered. She affects a coyness and lack of interest, by hitching herself sideways along the bottom of the aquarium, with her head turned over her right shoulder away from the swain. A trained ear might even detect her whistling in an indifferent manner.

The male, in the meantime, is flashing his gleamer frantically two blocks away and is performing all sorts of attractive feats, calculated to bring the lady newt to terms. I have seen a male, in the stress of his handicap courtship, stand on his fore-feet, gesticulating in amorous fashion with his hind feet in the air. Franz Ingehalt, in his " Über Weltschmerz des Newt," recounts having observed a distinct and deliberate undulation of the body, beginning with the shoulders and ending at the filament of the tail, which might well have been the origin of what is known to-day in scientific circles as " the shimmy." The object seems to be the same, except that in the case of the newt, it is the male who is the active agent.

In order to test the power of observation in the male during these manœuvers, I carefully removed the female, for whose benefit he was undulating, and put in her place, in slow succession, another (but

[6]

THE SOCIAL LIFE OF THE NEWT

less charming) female, a paper-weight of bronze shaped like a newt, and, finally, a common rubber eraser. From the distance at which the courtship was being carried on, the male (who was, it must be admitted, a bit near-sighted congenitally) was unable to detect the change in personnel, and continued, even in the presence of the rubber eraser, to gyrate and undulate in a most conscientious manner, still under the impression that he was making a conquest.

At last, worn out by his exertions, and disgusted at the meagerness of the reaction on the eraser, he gave a low cry of rage and despair and staggered to a nearby pan containing barley-water, from which he proceeded to drink himself into a gross stupor.

Thus, little creature, did your romance end, and who shall say that its ending was one whit less tragic than that of Camille? Not I, for one. . . . In fact, the two cases are not at all analogous.

And now that we have seen how wonderfully Nature works in the fulfilment of her laws, even among her tiniest creatures, let us study for a minute a cross-section of the community-life of the newt. It is a life full of all kinds of exciting adventure, from weaving nests to crawling about in the sun and catching insect larvæ and crustaceans. The newt's day is practically never done, largely because the insect larvæ multiply three million times as fast as the newt can possibly catch and eat them. And it takes the closest kind of community team-work in the newt colony to get things anywhere near cleaned up by nightfall.

It is early morning, and the workers are just appearing, hurrying to the old log which is to be the scene of their labors. What a scampering! What a bustle! Ah, little scamperers! Ah, little bustlers! How lucky you are, and how wise! You work long hours, without pay, for the sheer love of working. An ideal existence, I'll tell the scientific world.

Over here on the right of the log are the Master Draggers. Of all the newt workers, they are the most futile, which is high praise indeed. Come, let us look closer and see what it is that they are doing.

The one in the lead is dragging a bit of gurry out from the water and up over the edge into the sunlight. Following him, in single file, come the rest of the Master Draggers. They are not dragging anything, but are sort of helping the leader by crowding against him and eating little pieces out of the filament of his tail.

And now they have reached the top. The leader,

by dint of much leg-work, has succeeded in dragging his prize to the ridge of the log.

The little workers, reaching the goal with their precious freight, are now giving it over to the Master Pushers, who have been waiting for them in the sun all this while. The Master Pushers' work is soon accomplished, for it consists simply in pushing the piece of gurry over the other side of the log until it falls with a splash into the water, where it is lost.

This part of their day's task finished, the tiny toilers rest, clustered together in a group, waving their heads about from side to side, as who should say: " There—that's done! " And so it *is* done, my little Master Draggers and my little Master Pushers, and *well* done, too. Would that my own work were as clean-cut and as satisfying.

And so it goes. Day in and day out, the busy army of newts go on making the world a better place in which to live. They have their little trials and tragedies, it is true, but they also have their fun, as any one can tell by looking at a logful of sleeping newts on a hot summer day.

And, after all, what more has life to offer?

[9]

II

" COFFEE, MEGG AND ILK, PLEASE "

GIVE me any topic in current sociology, such as " The Working Classes *vs.* the Working Classes," or " Various Aspects of the Minimum Wage," and I can talk on it with considerable confidence. I have no hesitation in putting the Workingman, as such, in his place among the hewers of wood and drawers of water—a necessary adjunct to our modern life, if you will, but of little real consequence in the big events of the world.

But when I am confronted, in the flesh, by the " close up " of a workingman with any vestige of authority, however small, I immediately lose my perspective—and also my poise. I become servile, almost cringing. I feel that my modest demands on his time may, unless tactfully presented, be offensive to him and result in something, I haven't been able to analyze just what, perhaps public humiliation.

For instance, whenever I enter an elevator in a public building I am usually repeating to myself the number of the floor at which I wish to alight. The elevator man gives the impression of being a social worker, filling the job just for that day to help out the regular elevator man, and I feel that the least I can do is to show him that I know what's what. So I don't tell him my floor number as soon as I get in. Only elderly ladies do that. I keep whispering it over to myself, thinking to tell it to the world when the proper time comes. But then the big question arises—what is the proper time? If I want to get out at the eighteenth floor, should I tell him at the sixteenth or the seventeenth? I decide on the sixteenth and frame my lips to say, "Eighteen out, please." (Just why one should have to add the word "out" to the number of the floor is not clear. When you say "eighteen" the obvious construction of the phrase is that you want to get *out* at the eighteenth floor, not that you want to get *in* there or be let down through the flooring of the car at that point. However, you'll find the most sophisticated elevator riders, namely, messenger boys, always adding the word "out," and it is well to follow what the messenger boys do in such matters if you don't want to go wrong.)

So there I am, mouthing the phrase, "Eighteen out, please," as we shoot past the tenth—eleventh—twelfth—thirteenth floors. Then I begin to get panicky. Supposing that I should forget my lines! Or that I should say them too soon! Or too late!

We are now at the fifteenth floor. I clear my throat. Sixteen! Hoarsely I murmur, "Eighteen out." But at the same instant a man with a cigar in his mouth bawls, "Seventeen out!" and I am not heard.

"At the same instant a man with a cigar in his mouth bawls, 'Seventeen out!'"

The car stops at seventeen, and I step confidentially up to the elevator man and repeat, with an attempt at nonchalance, "Eighteen out, please." But just as I say the words the door clangs, drowning out my request, and we shoot up again. I make another attempt, but have become inarticulate and succeed only in making a noise like a man strangling. And by this time we are at the twenty-first floor with no relief in sight. Shattered, I retire to the back of the car and ride up to the roof and down again, trying to look as if I worked in the building and had to do it, however boresome it might be. On the return trip I don't care what the elevator man thinks of me, and tell him at every floor that I, personally, am going to get off at the eighteenth, no matter what any one else in the car does. I am dictatorial enough when I am riled. It is only in the opening rounds that I hug the ropes.

My timidity when dealing with minor officials strikes me first in my voice. I have any number of witnesses who will sign statements to the effect that my voice changed about twelve years ago, and that in ordinary conversation my tone, if not especially virile, is at least consistent and even. But when, for instance, I give an order at a soda fountain, if the clerk overawes me at all, my voice breaks into a yodel that makes the phrase "Coffee, egg and milk " a pretty snatch of song, but practically worthless as an order.

If the soda counter is lined with customers and the clerks so busy tearing up checks and dropping them into the toy banks that they seem to resent any call on their drink-mixing abilities, I might just as well save time and go home and shake up an egg and milk for myself, for I shall not be waited on until every one else has left the counter and they are putting the nets over the caramels for the night. I know that. I've gone through it too many times to be deceived.

For there is something about the realization that I must shout out my order ahead of some one else that absolutely inhibits my shouting powers. I will stand against the counter, fingering my ten-cent check and waiting for the clerk to come near enough for me to tell him what I want, while, in the meantime, ten or a dozen people have edged up next to me and given their orders, received their drinks and gone away. Every once in a while I catch a clerk's eye and lean forward murmuring, " Coffee " —but that is as far as I get. Some one else has shoved his way in and shouted, " Coca-Cola," and I draw back to get out of the way of the vichy spray. (Incidentally, the men who push their way in and footfault on their orders always ask for " Coca-Cola." Somehow it seems like painting the lily for them to order a nerve tonic.)

I then decide that the thing for me to do is to speak up loud and act brazenly. So I clear my throat, and, placing both hands on the counter, emit what promises to be a perfect bellow: " COFFEE,

" Placing both hands on the counter, I emit what promises to be
a perfect bellow."

MEGG AND ILK." This makes just about the impression you'd think it would, both on my neighbors and the clerk, especially as it is delivered in a tone which ranges from a rich barytone to a rather rasping tenor. At this I withdraw and go to the other end of the counter, where I can begin life over again with a clean slate.

Here, perhaps, I am suddenly confronted by an impatient clerk who is in a perfect frenzy to grab my check and tear it into bits to drop in his box. "What's yours?" he flings at me. I immediately lose my memory and forget what it was that I wanted. But here is a man who has a lot of people to wait on and who doubtless gets paid according to the volume of business he brings in. I have no right to interfere with his work. There is a big man edging his way beside me who is undoubtedly going to shout "Coca-Cola" in half a second. So I beat him to it and say, "Coca-Cola," which is probably the last drink in the store that I want to buy. But it is the only thing that I can remember at the moment, in spite of the fact that I have been thinking all morning how good a coffee, egg and milk would taste. I suppose that one of the psychological principles of advertising is to so hammer the name of your product into the mind of the timid buyer that when he is confronted by a brusk demand for an order he can't think of anything else to say, whether he wants it or not.

This dread of offending the minor official or appearing to a disadvantage before a clerk extends even to my taking nourishment. I don't think that I have ever yet gone into a restaurant and ordered exactly what I wanted. If only the waiter would give me the card and let me alone for, say, fifteen minutes, as he does when I want to get him to bring me my check, I could work out a meal along the lines of what I like. But when he stands over me, with disgust clearly registered on his face, I order the thing I like least and consider myself lucky to get out of it with so little disgrace.

And yet I have no doubt that if one could see him in his family life the Workingman is just an ordinary person like the rest of us. He is probably not at all as we think of him in our dealings with him—a harsh, dictatorial, intolerant autocrat, but rather a kindly soul who likes nothing better than to sit by the fire with his children and read.

And he would probably be the first person to scoff at the idea that he could frighten me.

III

WHEN GENIUS REMAINED YOUR
HUMBLE SERVANT

O F course, I really know nothing about it, but
I would be willing to wager that the last words
of Penelope, as Odysseus bounced down the front
steps, bag in hand, were: "Now, don't forget to
write, Odie. You'll find some papyrus rolled up
in your clean peplum, and just drop me a line on
it whenever you get a chance."

And ever since that time people have been prom-
ising to write, and then explaining why they haven't
written. Most personal correspondence of to-day
consists of letters the first half of which are given
over to an indexed statement of reasons why the
writer hasn't written before, followed by one paragraph of small talk, with the remainder devoted to
reasons why it is imperative that the letter be
brought to a close. So many people begin their
letters by saying that they have been rushed to death
during the last month, and therefore haven't found
time to write, that one wonders where all the grown
persons come from who attend movies at eleven in

[18]

the morning. There has been a misunderstanding of the word " busy " somewhere.

So explanatory has the method of letter writing become that it is probable that if Odysseus were a modern traveler his letters home to Penelope would average something like this:

Calypso,
Friday afternoon.

DEAR PEN:—I have been so tied up with work during the last week that I haven't had a chance to get near a desk to write to you. I have been trying to every day, but something would come up just at the last minute that would prevent me. Last Monday I got the papyrus all unrolled, and then I had to tend to Scylla and Charybdis (I may have written you about them before), and by the time I got through with them it was bedtime, and, believe me, I am snatching every bit of sleep I can get these days. And so it went, first the Læstrygones, and then something else, and here it is Friday. Well, there isn't much news to write about. Things are going along here about as usual. There is a young nymph here who seems to own the place, but I haven't had any chance to meet her socially. Well, there goes the ship's bell. I guess I had better be bringing this to a close. I have got a lot of work to do before I get dressed to go to a dinner of that nymph I was telling you about. I have met her brother, and he and I are interested in the same line of goods. He was at Troy with me. Well, I guess I must be closing. Will try to get off a longer letter in a day or two.

Your loving husband,

ODIE.

P.S.—You haven't got that bunch of sports hanging round the palace still, have you? Tell Telemachus I'll take him out of school if I hear of his playing around with any of them.

But there was a time when letter writing was such a fad, especially among the young girls, that if they had had to choose between eating three meals a day and writing a letter they wouldn't have given the meals even a consideration. In fact, they couldn't do both, for the length of maidenly letters in those days precluded any time out for meals. They may have knocked off for a few minutes during the heat of the day for a whiff at a bottle of salts, but to nibble at anything heartier than lettuce would have cramped their style.

Take Miss Clarissa Harlowe, for instance. In Richardson's book (which, in spite of my personal aversion to it, has been hailed by every great writer, from Pope to Stevenson, as being perfectly bully) she is given the opportunity of telling 2,400 closely printed pages full of story by means of letters to her female friend, Miss Howe (who plays a part similar to the orchestra leader in Frank Tinney's act). And 2,400 pages is nothing to her. When the book closes she is just beginning to get her stride. As soon as she got through with that she probably sat down and wrote a series of letters to the London papers about the need for conscription to fight the Indians in America.

To a girl like Clarissa, in the middle of the eighteenth century, no day was too full of horrors, no hour was too crowded with terrific happenings to prevent her from seating herself at a desk (she must have carried the desk about with her, strapped over her shoulder) and tearing off twenty or thirty pages to Friend Anna, telling her all about it. The only way that I can see in which she could accomplish this so efficiently would be to have a copy boy standing at her elbow, who took the letter, sheet by sheet, as she wrote it, and dashed with it to the printer.

It is hard to tell just which a girl of that period considered more important, the experiences she was writing of or the letter itself. She certainly never slighted the letter. If the experience wanted to overtake her, and jump up on the desk beside her, all right, but, experience or no experience, she was going to get that letter in the next post or die in the attempt. Unfortunately, she never died in the attempt.

Thus, an attack on a young lady's house by a band of cutthroats, resulting in the burning of the structure and her abduction, might have been told of in the eighteenth century letter system as follows:

Monday night.

SWEET ANNA:—At this writing I find myself in the most horrible circumstance imaginable. Picture to yourself, if you can, my dear Anna, a party of villainous brigands, veritable cutthroats, all of them, led by a surly fellow in green alpaca with white insertion, breaking their way, by very force, through the side of your domicile, like so many ugly intruders, and threatening you with vile imprecations to make you disclose the hiding place of the family jewels. If the mere thought of such a contingency is painful to you, my beloved Anna, consider what it means to me, your delicate friend, to whom it is actually happening at this very minute! For such is in very truth the situation which is disclosing itself in my room as I write. Not three feet away from me is the odious person before described. Now he is threatening me with renewed vigor! Now he has placed his coarse hands on my throat, completely hiding the pearl necklace which papa brought me from Epsom last summer, and which you, and also young Pindleson (whose very name I mention with a blush), have so often admired. But more of this later, and until then, believe me, my dear Anna, to be

Your ever distressed and affectionate

CL. HARLOWE.

Monday night. Later.

DEAREST ANNA:—Now, indeed, it is evident, my best, my only friend, that I am face to face with the bitterest of fates. You will remember that in my last letter I spoke to you of a party of unprincipled knaves who were invading my apartment. And now do I find that they have, in furtherance of their inexcusable plans, set fire to that portion of the house which lies directly behind this, so that as I put my pen to paper the flames are creeping, like hungry creatures of some sort, through the partitions and into this very room, so that did I esteem my safety more than my correspondence with you, my precious companion, I should at once be making preparation for immediate departure. O my dear! To be thus seized, as I am at this very

[23]

"To be thus seized . . . is truly, you will agree, my sweet Anna, a pitiable episode."

instant, by the unscrupulous leader of the band and carried, by brute force, down the stairway through the butler's pantry and into the servants' hall, writing as I go, resting my poor paper on the shoulder of my detested abductor, is truly, you will agree, my sweet Anna, a pitiable episode.

Adieu, my intimate friend.

Your obt. s'v't,

CL. HARLOWE.

One wonders (or, at least, *I* wonder, and that is sufficient for the purposes of this article) what the letter writing young lady of that period would have done had she lived in this day of postcards showing the rocks at Scipawisset or the Free Public Library in East Tarvia. She might have used them for some of her shorter messages, but I rather doubt it. The foregoing scene could hardly have been done justice to on a card bearing the picture of the Main Street of the town, looking north from the Soldiers' Monument, with the following legend:

" Our house is the third on the left with the lilac bush. Cross marks window where gang of roughnecks have just broken in and are robbing and burning the house. Looks like a bad night. Wish you were here. " C. H."

No; that would never have done, but it would have been a big relief for the postilion, or whoever it was that had to carry Miss Clarissa's effusions to their destination. The mail on Monday morning, after a springlike Sunday, must have been something in the nature of a wagon load of rolls of news print that used to be seen standing in front of newspaper offices in the good old days when newspapers were printed on paper stock. Of course, the postilion had the opportunity of whiling away the time between stations by reading some of the spicier bits in the assortment, but even a postilion must have had his feelings, and a man can't read that kind of stuff *all* of the time, and still keep his health.

Of course, there are a great many people now who write letters because they like to. Also, there are some who do it because they feel that they owe it to posterity and to their publishers to do so. As soon as a man begins to sniff a chance that he may become moderately famous he is apt to brush up on his letter writing and never send anything out that has not been polished and proofread, with the idea in mind that some day some one is going to get all of his letters together and make a book of them. Apparently, most great men whose letters have been published have had premonition of their greatness when quite young, as their childish letters bear the marks of careful and studied attention to publicity values. One can almost imagine the budding genius, aged eight, sitting at his desk and saying to himself:

"I must not forget that I am now going through the '*Sturm und Drang*' period."

"In this spontaneous letter to my father I must not forget that I am now going through the *Sturm und Drang* (storm and stress) period of my youth and that this letter will have to be grouped by the compiler under the *Sturm und Drang* (storm and stress) section in my collected letters. I must therefore keep in the key and quote only such of my fa-

[27]

vorite authors as will contribute to the effect. I
think I will use Werther to-day. . . . My dear Father "—etc.

I have not known many geniuses in their youth,
but I have had several youths pointed out to me
by their parents as geniuses, and I must confess
that I have never seen a letter from any one of them
that differed greatly from the letters of a normal
boy, unless perhaps they were spelled less accurately.
Given certain uninteresting conditions, let us say,
at boarding school, and I believe that the average
bright boy's letter home would read something in
this fashion:

> *Exeter, N. H.,*
> *Wed., April 25.*

MY DEAR FATHER AND MOTHER:

I have been working pretty hard this week, studying for a history examination, and so haven't had
much of a chance to write to you. Everything is
about the same as usual here, and there doesn't
seem to be much news to write to you about. The
box came all right, and thank you very much. All
the fellows liked it, especially the little apple pies.
Thank you very much for sending it. There hasn't
much been happening here since I wrote you last
week. I had to buy a new pair of running drawers,

which cost me fifty cents. Does that come out of my allowance? Or will you pay for it? There doesn't seem to be any other news. Well, there goes the bell, so I guess I will be closing.

Your loving son,
BUXTON.

Given the same, even less interesting conditions, and a boy such as Stevenson must have been (judging from his letters) could probably have delivered himself of this, and more, too:

Wyckham-Wyckham,
The Tenth.

DEAR PATER:—To-day has been unbelievably exquisite! Great, undulating clouds, rolling in serried formation across a sky of pure *lapis lazuli*. I feel like what Updike calls a " myrmidon of unhesitating amplitude." And a perfect gem of a letter from Toto completed the felicitous experience. You would hardly believe, and yet you must, in your *cœur des cœurs*, know, that the brown, esoteric hills of this Oriental retreat affect me like the red wine of Russilon, and, indigent as I am in these matters, I cannot but feel that you have, as Herbert says:

> " *Carve or discourse; do not a famine fear.*
> *Who carves is kind to two, who talks to all.*"

Yesterday I saw a little native boy, a veritable boy of the streets, playing at a game at once so naïve and so resplendent that I was irresistibly drawn to its contemplation. You will doubtless jeer when I tell you. He was tossing a small *blatch*, such as grow in great profusion here, to and fro between himself and the wall of the *limple*. I was stunned for the moment, and then I realized that I was looking into the very soul of the peasantry, the open stigma of the nation. How queer it all seemed! Did it not?

You doubtless think me an ungrateful fellow for not mentioning the delicious assortment of goodies which came, like melons to Artemis, to this benighted *gesellschaft* on Thursday last. They were devoured to the last crumb, and I was reminded as we ate, like so many *wurras*, of those lines of that gorgeous Herbert, of whom I am so fond:

> " *Must all be veiled, while he that reads divines,*
> *Catching the sense at two removes?* "

The breeze is springing up, and it brings to me messages of the open meadows of Litzel, deep festooned with the riot of gloriannas. How quiet they seem to me as I think of them now! How emblematic! Do you know, my dear Parent, that I sometimes wonder if, after all, it were not better to dream, and dream . . . and dream.

Your affectionate son,

BERGQUIST.

So don't worry about your boy if he writes home like that. He may simply have an eye for fame and future compilation.

IV

THE TORTURES OF WEEK-END VISITING

THE present labor situation shows to what a pretty pass things may come because of a lack of understanding between the parties involved. I bring in the present labor situation just to give a touch of timeliness to this thing. Had I been writing for the Christmas number, I should have begun as follows: " The indiscriminate giving of Christmas presents shows to what a pretty pass things may come because of a lack of understanding between the parties involved."

The idea to be driven home is that things may come to a pretty pass by the parties involved in an affair of any kind if they do not come to an understanding before commencing operations.

I hope I have made my point clear. Especially is this true, (watch out carefully now, as the whole nub of the article will be coming along in just a minute), especially is this true in the relations between host and guest on week-end visits. (There, you have it! In fact, the title to this whole thing might very well be, " The Need for a Clearer Definition of Relations between Host and Guest on Week-end Visits," and not be at all overstating it, at that.)

The logic of this will be apparent to any one who has ever been a host or a guest at a week-end party, a classification embracing practically all Caucasians over eleven years of age who can put powder on the nose or tie a bow-tie. Who has not wished that his host would come out frankly at the beginning of the visit and state, in no uncertain terms, the rules and preferences of the household in such matters as the breakfast hour? And who has not sounded his guest to find out what he likes in the regulation of his diet and *modus vivendi* (mode of living)? Collective bargaining on the part of labor unions and capital makes it possible for employers to know just what the workers think on matters of common interest. Is collective bargaining between host and guest so impossible, then?

Take, for example, the matter of arising in the morning. Of course, where there is a large house-party the problem is a simple one, for you can always hear the others pattering about and brushing their teeth. You can regulate your own arising by the number of people who seem to be astir. But if you are the only guest there is apt to be a frightful misunderstanding.

"At what time is breakfast?" you ask.

"Oh, any old time on Sundays," replies the hostess with a generous gesture. "Sleep as late as you like. This is 'Liberty Hall.'"

The sentiment in this attitude is perfectly bully, but there is nothing that you can really take hold of in it. It satisfies at the time, but in the morning there is a vagueness about it that is simply terrifying.

Let us say that you awake at eight. You listen and hear no one stirring. Then, over on the cool pillow again until eight-twenty. Again up on the elbow, with head cocked on one side. There is a creak in the direction of the stairs. They may all be up and going down to breakfast! It is but the work of a moment, to bound out of bed and listen at the door. Perhaps open it modestly and peer out. Deathlike silence, broken only, as the phrase goes, by the ticking of the hall clock, and not a soul in sight. Probably they are late sleepers. Maybe eleven o'clock is their Sunday rising hour. Some people *are* like that.

Shut the door and sit on the edge of the bed. More sleep is out of the question. Let's take a look at the pictures in the guest-room, just to pass the time. Here's one of Lorna Doone. How d'e do, Lorna? Here's a group—taken in 1902—showing

[34]

your host in evening clothes, holding a mandolin. Probably a member of his college musical-club. Rather unkempt looking bunch, you *must* say. Well, how about this one? An etching, showing suspicious-looking barges on what is probably the Thames. Fair enough, at that.

Back to the door and listen again. Tick-tock-tick-tock. Probably, if you started your tub, you'd wake the whole house. Let's sit down on the edge of the bed again.

Hello, here are some books on the table. " Fifty Famous Sonnets," illustrated by Maxfield Parrish. Never touch a sonnet before breakfast. " My experiences in the Alps," by a woman mountain-climber who has written on the fly-leaf, " To my good friends the Elbridges, in memory of many happy days together at Chamounix. October, 1907." That settles *that*. " Essay on Compensation " in limp leather, by R. W. Emerson, published by Houghton, Mifflin & Co. Oh, very well! You suppose they thought that would be over your head, did they? Well, we'll just show them! We'll read it just for spite. Opening, to the red ribbon:

" Of the like nature is that expectation of change which instantly follows the suspension of our voluntary activity. The terror of cloudless noon—"

By the way, it must be nearly noon now! Ten

minutes past nine, only! Well, the only thing to do is get dressed and go out and walk about the grounds. Eliminate the tub as too noisy. And so, very cautiously, almost clandestinely, you proceed to dress.

And now, just to reverse the process. Suppose you are the host. You have arisen at eight and listened at the guest's door. No sound. Tip-toe back and get dressed, talking in whispers to your wife (the hostess) and cramming flannel bears into the infant's mouth to keep him from disturbing the sleeper.

" Bill looked tired last night. Better let him sleep a little longer," you suggest. And so, downstairs on your hands and knees, and look over the Sunday papers. Then a bracing walk on the porch, resulting in a terrific appetite.

A glance at the watch shows nine o'clock. Sunday breakfast is usually at eight-thirty. The warm aroma of coffee creeps in from the kitchen and, somewhere, *some one* is baking muffins. This is awful! You suppose it feels something like this to be caught on an ice-floe without any food and so starve to death. Only there you can't smell coffee and muffins. You sneak into the dining-room and steal one of the property oranges from the sideboard, but little Edgar sees you and sets up such a howl that you have to give it to him. The hostess suggests that your friend may have the sleeping-sickness. Weakened by hunger, you hotly resent this, and one word leads to another.

" Oh, very well, I'll go up and rout him out," you snarl.

Upstairs again, and poise, in listening attitude,

" ' Hello, Bill,' you say flatly."

just in front of the guest's door. Slowly the door opens, inch by inch, and, finally his head is edged cautiously out toward yours.

" Hello, Bill," you say flatly, " what are you getting up this time of the morning for? Thought I told you to sleep late."

" Morning, Ed," he says, equally flatly, " hope

[37]

I haven't kept you all waiting." Then you both lie and eat breakfast.

Such a misunderstanding is apt to go to almost any length. I once knew of a man on a week-end visit who spent an entire Sunday in his room, listening at his door to see if the family were astir, while, in the meantime, the family were, one by one, tip-toeing to his door to see if they could detect any signs of life from him.

Each thought the other needed rest.

Along about three in the afternoon the family threw all hospitality aside and ate breakfast, deadening the sound of the cutlery as much as possible, little dreaming that their guest was looking through the " A Prayer for Each Day " calendar for the ninth time and seriously considering letting himself down from the window on a sheet and making for the next train. Shortly after dark persistent rumors got abroad that he had done away with himself, and every one went up and sniffed for gas. It was only when the maid, who was not in on the secret, bolted into the room to turn down his bed for the night, that she found him tip-toeing about, packing and unpacking his bag and listening eagerly at the wall. (Now don't ask how it happened that the maid didn't know that his bed hadn't been made that morning. What difference does it make, anyway? It is such questions as *that,* that blight any attempt at individual writing in this country.)

Don't think, just because I have taken all this space to deal with the rising-hour problem that there are no other points to be made. Oh, not at all. There is, for instance, the question of exercise. After dinner the host says to himself: "Something must be done. I wonder if he likes to walk." Aloud, he says: "Well, Bill, how about a little hike in the country? "

A hike in the country being the last thing in the world that Bill wants, he says, "Right-o! Anything you say." And so, although walking is a tremendous trial to the host, who has weak ankles, he bundles up with a great show of heartiness and grabs his stick as if this were the one thing he lived for.

After about a mile of hobbling along the country-road the host says, hopefully: "Don't let me tire you out, old man. Any time you want to turn back, just say the word."

The guest, thinking longingly of the fireside, scoffs at the idea of turning back, insisting that if there is one thing in all the world that he likes better than walking it is running. So on they jog, hippity-hop, hippity-hop, each wishing that it would rain so that they could turn about and go home.

Here again the thing may go to almost tragic

[39]

lengths. Suppose neither has the courage to suggest the return move. They might walk on into Canada, or they might become exhausted and have to be taken into a roadhouse and eat a "$2 old-fashioned Southern dinner of fried chicken and waffles." The imagination revolts at a further contem-

"So on they jog. . . . Each wishing that it would rain."

plation of the possibilities of this lack of coöperation between guest and host.

I once visited a man who had an outdoor swimming-pool on his estate. (Consider that as very casually said.) It was in April, long before Spring had really understood what was expected of her. My first night there my host said:

"Are you a morning plunger?"

THE TORTURES OF VISITING

Thinking that he referred to a tub plunge in a warm bathroom, I glowed and said: " You bet."

" I'll call for you at seven in the morning, then," he said, " and we'll go out to the pool."

It was evidently his morning custom and I wasn't going to have it said of me that a middle-aged man could outdo me in virility. So, at seven in the morning, in a dense fog (with now and then a slash of cold rain), we picked our way out to the pool and staged a vivid Siberian moving picture scene, showing naked peasants bathing in the Nevsky. My visit lasted five days, and I afterward learned, from one to whom my host had confided, that it was the worst five days he had ever gone through, and that he has chronic joint-trouble as a result of those plunges. " But I couldn't be outdone by a mere stripling," he said, " and the boy certainly enjoyed it."

All of this might have been avoided by the posting of a sign in a conspicuous place in my bedroom, reading as follows: " Personally, I dislike swimming in the pool at this time of the year. Guests wishing to do so may obtain towels at the desk." How very simple and practical!

The sign system is the only solution I can offer. It is crude and brutal, but it admits of no misunderstanding. A sign in each guest-room, giving the hours of meals, political and religious preferences of the family, general views on exercise, etc., etc., with a blank for the guest to fill out, stating his own views on these subjects, would make it possible to visit (or entertain) with a sense of security thus far unknown upon our planet.

V

GARDENING NOTES

DURING the past month almost every paper, with the exception of the agricultural journals, has installed an agricultural department, containing short articles by Lord Northcliffe, or some one else in the office who had an unoccupied typewriter, telling the American citizen how to start and hold the interest of a small garden. The seed catalogue has become the catechism of the patriot, and, if you don't like to read the brusk, prosy directions on planting as given there, you may find the same thing done in verse in your favorite poetry magazine, or a special department in *The Plumbing Age* under the heading "The Plumber's Garden: How and When to Plant."

But all of these editorial suggestions appear to be conducted by professionals for the benefit of the layman, which seems to me to be a rather one-sided way of going about the thing. Obviously the suggestions should come from a layman himself, in the nature of warnings to others.

I am qualified to put forth such an article because of two weeks' service in my own back yard, doing my bit for Peter Henderson and planting all sorts of things in the ground without the slightest expectation of ever seeing anything of any' of them again. If, by any chance, a sprout should show itself, unmistakably the result of one of my plantings, I would be willing to be quoted as saying that Nature *is* wonderful. In fact, I would take it as a personal favor, and would feel that anything that I might do in the future for Nature would be little enough in return for the special work she went to all the trouble of doing for me. But all of this is on condition that something of mine grows into manhood. Otherwise, Nature can go her way and I'll go mine, just as we have gone up till now.

However, although I am an amateur, I shall have to adopt, in my writing, the tone of a professional, or I shall never get any one to believe what I say. If, therefore, from now on I sound a bit cold and unfriendly, you will realize that a professional agricultural writer has to have *some* dignity about his stuff, and that beneath my rough exterior I am a pleasant enough sort of person to meet socially.

Preparing the Ground for the Garden

This is one of the most important things that the young gardener is called upon to do. In fact, a great many young gardeners never do anything further. Some inherited weakness, something **they** never realized they had before, may crop out during this process: weak back, tendency of shoulder-

"If you are able to walk as far as the bathtub . . ."

blades to ossification, misplacement of several important vertebrae, all are apt to be discovered for the first time during the course of one day's digging. If, on the morning following the first attempt to prepare the ground for planting, you are able to walk in a semi-erect position as far as the bath-tub (and, without outside assistance, lift one foot into the water), you may flatter yourself that you are,

[45]

joint for joint, in as perfect condition as the man in the rubber-heels advertisements.

Authorities differ as to the best way of digging. All agree that it is impossible to avoid walking about during the following week as if you were impersonating an old colored waiter with the lumbago; but there are two schools, each with its own theory, as to the less painful method. One advocates bending over, without once raising up, until the whole row is dug. The others, of whom I must confess that I am one, feel that it is better to draw the body to a more or less erect position after each shovelful. In support of this contention, Greitz, the well-known authority on the muscles of the back, says on page 233 of his " Untersuchungen über Sittlichkeitsdelikte und Gesellschaftsbiologie ":

" The constant tightening and relaxing of the *latissimus dorsi* effected in raising the body as the earth is tossed aside, has a tendency to relieve the strain by distributing it equally among the *serratus posticus inferior* and the corner of Thirty-fourth Street." He then goes on to say practically what I have said above.

The necessity for work of such a strenuous nature in the mere preliminaries of the process of planting a garden is due to the fact that the average back-yard has, up till the present time, been

[46]

behaving less like a garden than anything else in the world. You might think that a back-yard, possessed of an ordinary amount of decency and civic-pride would, at some time during its career, have said to itself:

"Now look here! I may some day be called upon to be a garden, and the least I can do is to get myself into some sort of shape, so that, when the time comes, I will be fairly ready to receive a seed or two."

But no! Year in and year out they have been drifting along in a fools' paradise, accumulating stones and queer, indistinguishable cans and things, until they were prepared to become anything, quarries, iron-mines, notion-counters,—anything but gardens.

I have saved in a box all the things that I have dug from my back-yard, and, when I have them assembled, all I will need will be a good engine to make them into a pretty fairly decent runabout,— nothing elaborate, mind you, but good enough to run the family out in on Sunday afternoons.

And then there are lots of other things that wouldn't even fit into the runabout. Queer-looking objects, they are; things that perhaps in their heyday were rather stunning, but which have now assumed an air of indifference, as if to say, " Oh, call me anything, old fellow, Ice-pick, Mainspring, Cigar-lighter, anything, I don't care." I tell you, it's enough to make a man stop and think. But there, I mustn't get sentimental.

In preparing the soil for planting, you will need several tools. Dynamite would be a beautiful thing to use, but it would have a tendency to get the dirt into the front-hall and track up the stairs. This not being practicable, there is no other way but for you to get at it with a fork (oh, don' be silly), a spade, and a rake. If you have an empty and detached furnace boiler, you might bring that along to fill with the stones you will dig up. If it is a small garden, you ought not to have to empty the boiler more than three or four times. Any neighbor who is building a stone house will be glad to contract with you for the stones, and those that are left over after he has got his house built can be sold to another neighbor who is building another stone house. Your market is limited only by the number of neighbors who are building stone houses.

On the first day, when you find yourself confronted by a stretch of untouched ground which is to be turned over (technical phrase, meaning to "turn over"), you may be somewhat at a loss to know where to begin. Such indecision is only natural, and should cause no worry on the part of the young gardener. It is something we all have to go through with. You may feel that it would be futile and unsystematic to go about digging up a forkful here and a shovelful there, tossing the earth at random, in the hope that in due time you will get the place dug up. And so it would.

The thing to do is to decide just where you want your garden, and what its dimensions are to be. This will have necessitated a previous drawing up of a chart, showing just what is to be planted and where. As this chart will be the cause of considerable hard feeling in the family circle, usually precipitating a fist-fight over the number of rows of onions to be set out, I will not touch on that in this article. There are some things too intimate for even a professional agriculturist to write of. I will say, however, that those in the family who are standing out for onions might much better save their time and feelings by pretending to give in, and then, later in the day, sneaking out and slipping the sprouts in by themselves in some spot where they will know where to find them again.

Having decided on the general plan and dimensions of the plot, gather the family about as if for a corner-stone dedication, and then make a rather impressive ceremony of driving in the first stake by

[49]

getting your little boy to sing the first twelve words
of some patriotic air. (If he doesn't know the first
twelve, any twelve will do. The idea is to keep the
music going during the driving of the stake.)

"Make a rather impressive ceremony of driving the first stake."

The stake is to be driven at an imaginary corner
of what is to be your garden, and a string stretched
to another stake at another imaginary corner, and
there you have a line along which to dig. This
will be a big comfort. You will feel that at last
you have something tangible. Now all that remains
is to turn the ground over, harrow it, smooth it up

nice and neat, plant your seeds, cultivate them, thin out your plants and pick the crops.

It may seem that I have spent most of my time in advice on preparing the ground for planting. Such may well be the case, as that was as far as I got. I then found a man who likes to do those things and whose doctor has told him that he ought to be out of doors all the time. He is an Italian, and charges really very little when you consider what he accomplishes. Any further advice on starting and keeping up a garden, I shall have to get him to write for you.

VI

LESSON NUMBER ONE

FRANKLY, I am not much of a hand at machinery of any sort. I have no prejudice against it as such, for some of my best friends are of a mechanical turn of mind, and very nice fellows they are too. But the pencil sharpener in our office is about as far as I, personally, have ever got in the line of operating a complicated piece of mechanism with any degree of success.

So, when George suggested that he teach me to run his car, it seemed a reasonable proposition. Obviously, *some one* had to teach me. I couldn't be expected to go out and pick the thing up by myself, like learning to eat olives. No matter how well-intentioned I might be, or how long I stuck at it, the chances are that I never could learn to drive a car simply by sitting in the seat alone and fooling around among the gadgets until I found the right ones. Something would be sure to happen to spoil the whole thing long before I got the hang of it.

LESSON NUMBER ONE

The car was, therefore, brought out into the driveway at the side of the house, like a bull being led into the ring for a humid afternoon with the matador. It was right here that George began to show his true colors, for he stopped the engine, which was running very nicely as it was, and said that I might as well begin by learning to crank it, as I probably would spend seven-eighths of my driving time cranking in the future.

I didn't like this in George. It showed that he wasn't going about it in the right spirit. He was beginning with the assumption that I would make a dub of myself, and, as I was already beginning to assume the same thing, it looked rather black for the lesson, with both parties to it holding the same pessimistic thought.

So, right off the bat, I said:

"No, George. It seems to me that you ought to crank it yourself. To-day I am learning to *drive* the car. 'One thing at a time' is my motto. That is what has brought our modern industrial system to its present state of efficiency: the Division of Labor—one man who does nothing but make holes in washers, another who does nothing but slip the washers over the dinguses over which they belong; one man who devotes his whole time to running a car, another who specializes in cranking it. Now, in the early days of industry, when the guild was the unit of organization among the workers—"

George, having cranked the engine, motioned me into the driver's seat, and took his position beside me. It struck me that the thing was very poorly arranged, in that the place which was to be occupied by the driver, obviously the most important person in the car (except, of course, the lady member of the party in the tonneau, who holds the bluebook and gives wrong directions as to turnings), was all cluttered up with a lot of apparatus and pedals and things, so much so that I had to inhale and contract in order to squeeze past the wheel into my seat. And even then I was forced to stretch one leg out so far that I kicked a little gadget on a box arrangement on the dashboard, which apparently stopped the engine. As he cranked it again, George said, among other things, that it couldn't possibly have been done except on purpose, and that he could take a joke as well as the next man, but that, good night, what was the use of being an ass?

As if I, with no mechanical instinct whatever, knew what was in that box! I don't know even now, and I have got my driver's license.

George finally got things stirring again and climbed in, leaving the door partly open—no doubt in order that, in case of emergency, he could walk, not run, to the street via the nearest exit.

"The gear set of this car is of the planetary type," he said, by way of opening the seminar, while the motor behaved as if it were trying to jiggle

" George said that he could take a joke, but that, good night! what was the use of being an ass? "

its way out from under the cushions and bite me. "This planetary system gives two forward speeds and a reverse motion."

"Nothing could be fairer than that. It sounds like an almost perfect arrangement to me," I said, to show that I was listening. And then, to show that I was thinking about the thing as well, I asked: " But surely you don't have to pedal the thing along yourself by foot power! All those pedals down there would seem to leave very little for the gasoline power to do."

"Those three pedals are what do the trick," explained George. And then he added ominously: "If you should step on that left-hand one now, you would throw in your clutch."

"Please, George, don't get morbid," I protested. "I'm nervous enough as it is, without having to worry about my own bodily safety."

"The middle pedal, marked 'R,' is the reverse, and the one at the right, marked 'B,' is the foot brake. Now, when you want to start—"

"Just a minute, please," I said sternly. "You skip over those as if there were something about them you were a little ashamed of, George. Are you keeping something from me about the reverse and the foot brake?"

"I didn't know but that somewhere in your valuable college course they taught you what 'reverse' meant, and I was sure that your little son had told you all about the foot brake on his express wagon," said George, waxing sarcastic in the manner of the technical man that he is.

"I don't want you to take anything for granted in teaching me to run this thing," I replied. "It is those little things that count, you know, and I would feel just as badly as you would if I were to run your car over a cliff into a rocky gorge because of some detail that I was uninformed about. You know that, George."

"Very well," he said, "I'll get down to fundamentals. When you push the reverse pedal, you drive the car in the opposite direction from that in which it is headed. This is done by tightening the external contracting clutch bands which are between the gearing and the disk clutch."

Somehow this struck me as funny. The idea of reversing by tightening *any* bands at all, much less external contracting ones, was the one thing needed to send me off into roars of laughter. The whole thing seemed so flat, after the excitement of the war, and everything.

Naturally George didn't get it. It was 'way over his head, and I knew that there would be no use trying to explain it to him. So I just continued to chuckle and murmur: "External contracting clutch bands! You'll be the death of me yet, George!"

But I felt that, as the minutes went by, the situation was getting strained. My instructor and I were growing farther and farther apart in spirit, and, after all, it was his car and he was going to considerable trouble to teach me to run it, and the least that I could do would be to take him seriously,

[57]

whether the thing struck me as being sensible or not.

So I calmed myself with some effort, and tried to bring the conversation around to an opening for him to begin with further explanations.

" But, all joking aside, George, how can you be so sure about these things? You say that when you push the reverse pedal you tighten the external contracting clutch bands. Did you ever *see* them tighten? Or are you taking some one's word for it? Remember how the German people were deceived for years by their rulers! Now supposing—just supposing—that it had been to some unscrupulous person's advantage to make you think that the—"

" Now, listen, Bob," said George (my name *is* Bob, and I see no reason why, simply because I am writing a piece about myself, I should make believe that my name is Stuart or Will, especially as it is right there in black and white at the head of the story. This assuming new names on the part of authors is a literary affectation which ought to be done away with once and for all). " Now, listen, Bob," said George, very quietly and very distinctly, " the only thing for you to do if you are going to learn to run this thing, is to get right down to brass tacks and *run* it, and the sooner you try it, the better."

" Oh, you practical guys! " I said. " Nothing will

do but you must always be getting down to brass tacks. It's men like you who are driving all the poetry out of the world."

"You flatter me," said George, reaching bruskly across me as if he were after the salt and pepper, and adjusting a couple of dingbats on the steering wheel. "This here is the spark, and this is the throttle. The throttle governs the gas supply, and the spark regulates the—eh, well, it regulates the spark."

"What won't these scientists think up next?" I marveled. "It's uncanny, that's what it is—uncanny."

"*Now,* then: hold your foot on the clutch pedal and keep her in neutral, while you shove your hand lever forward as far as it will go. *That's* right! . . . That's fine . . . 'way forward . . . now . . . *that's* right . . . that's fine!"

I was so encouraged by the way things seemed to be going that I took all my feet away from all the things they were stepping on, and sighed:

"Let's rest a minute, old man. I'm all of a tremble. It's much easier than I thought, but I'd rather take it stage by stage than to dash right off the first thing."

The trouble seemed to be that, in lifting my feet, I had discouraged the motor, which sighed and stopped functioning, giving the car a playful shake, like an Erie local stopping at Babbitt (N. J.) on signal. So George said that, in the future, no matter how well things seemed to be going, never to give in to my emotions again, but keep right on working, even though it looked as if I were in danger of becoming an expert driver in three minutes. There is always something to learn, he said. Then he got out and cranked the engine.

We went through the same process again, only I kept my foot on the vox humana pedal until I had crammed it 'way into fortissimo. Then suddenly a wonderful thing happened. The whole thing—car, engine, George, and I—began to move, all together. It was a big moment in my life. I could see the headlines in the evening papers:

YOUNG SCRIBE OVERCOMES NATURAL LAWS
Causes Auto to Move by Pushing Pedal

But this elation was for only a moment. For, while we had been arguing, some one had sneaked up in front of us and transplanted the hydrangea bush from the lawn at our side to the very middle of the driveway, a silly place for a hydrangea bush at best, but an absolutely fatal one at the moment when an automobile was being driven through the yard.

LESSON NUMBER ONE

It was but the work of a second for me to sense the danger. It was but the work of *half* a second, however, for us to be rustling our way slowly and lumberingly into the luxuriant foliage of the bush. So I was just about half a second late, which I do not consider bad for a beginner.

" Put on your brake! " shouted George.

Quick as a wink (one of those long sensuous winks) I figured out which the brake was, by finding the symbolical " B " on the pedal. Like a trained mechanician I stepped on it.

" Release your clutch first, you poor fish! " screamed George, above the horrible grinding noise. " Release your clutch! "

This was more than flesh and blood could bear. Again I relieved my feet from any responsibility in the affair, and turned to my instructor.

" Don't *shout* so! " I yelled back at him. " And don't keep calling it *my* clutch! It may be because I was brought up in a Puritan family, but the whole subject of clutches is a closed book to me. If it is something I should know about, you can tell me when we get in the house. But, for the present, let's drop the matter. At any rate, I stopped your darn car, clutch, or no clutch."

And so I had. There we were, in the middle of the hydrangea bush, very quiet and peaceful, like a couple of birds in a bird house atop of rustling oak (or maple, for that matter). Even the engine had stopped.

I reached out and plucked a blossom that was peeking over the dashboard where the whip socket should have been. After all, there is no place like the country. I said so to George, and he tacitly agreed. At least, I took it to be agreement. It was certainly tacit. I was afraid that he was a little hurt over what I had said about the clutch, and so I decided that it might be best not to mention the subject again. In fact, it seemed wiser to get away from the topic of automobiles entirely. So I said softly:

" George, did it ever occur to you how the war has changed our daily life? Not only have we had to alter our methods of provisioning our tables and feeding our families, but we have acquired a certain detachment of mind, a certain new sufficiency of spirit."

(We had both alighted from the car and had placed ourselves, one on each side, to roll it out of the embraces of the hydrangea bush.)

" I have been reading a book during the past week on Problems of Reconstruction," I continued, " and I have been impressed by the thought which

LESSON NUMBER ONE

"After all, there is no place like the country. I said so to
George, and he tacitly agreed."

is being given to the development of the waste lands in the West."

(We had, by this time, got the car rolled out into the driveway again.)

"The problem of the children, too, is an absorbing one for the years which lie ahead of us. We cannot go back to the old methods of child training, any more than we can go back to the old methods of diplomacy. The war has created a hiatus. That which follows will depend on the zeal with which America applies herself to her task of rehabilitation."

(The machine was now moored in her parking space by the porte-cochère, and the brakes applied.)

"It seems to me that we are living in a great period of transition; doesn't it look that way to you, George?"

"Yes," said George.

And so we went into the house.

VII

THOUGHTS ON FUEL SAVING

CONSIDERABLE space has been given in the magazines and newspapers this winter to official and expert directions on How to Run Your Furnace and Save Coal—as if the two things were compatible. Some had accompanying diagrams of a furnace in its normal state, showing the exact position of the arteries and vitals, with arrows pointing in interesting directions, indicating the theoretical course of the heat.

I have given some time to studying these charts, and have come to the conclusion that when the authors of such articles and I speak the word " furnace," we mean entirely different things. They are referring to some idealized, sublimated creation; perhaps the " furnace " which existed originally in the mind of Horace W. Furnace, the inventor; while, on the other hand, I am referring to the thing that is in my cellar. No wonder that I can't understand their diagrams.

For my own satisfaction, therefore, I have drawn up a few regulations which I *can* understand, and

[65]

have thrown them together most informally for whatever they may be worth. Any one else who has checked up the official furnace instructions with Life as it really is and has found something wrong somewhere may go as far as he likes with the results of my researches. I give them to the world.

Saving coal is, just now, the chief concern of most householders, for we are now entering that portion of the solstice when it is beginning to be necessary to walk some distance into the bin after the coal. When first the list of official admonitions were issued, early in the season, it was hard to believe that they ever would be needed. The bin was so full that it resembled a drug-store window piled high with salted peanuts. (As a matter of actual fact, there is probably nothing that coal looks *less* like than salted peanuts, but the effect of tremendous quantity was the same.) Adventurous pieces were fairly popping out of confinement and rolling over the cellar. It seemed as if there were enough coal there to give the *Leviathan* a good run for her money and perhaps take her out as far as Bedloe Island. A fig for coal-saving devices!

But now the season is well on, and the bad news is only too apparent. The householder, as he finds himself walking farther and farther into the bin after the next shovelful, realizes that soon will come the time when it will be necessary to scrape the leavings into a corner, up against the side of the bin, and to coal his fire, piece by piece, between his finger and thumb, while waiting for the dealer to deliver that next load, "right away, probably to-day, to-morrow at the latest."

It is therefore essential that we turn constructive thought to the subject of coal conservation. I would suggest, in the first place, an exact aim in shoveling coal into the fire box.

By this I mean the cultivation of an exact aim in shoveling coal into the fire box. In my own case (if I may be permitted to inject the personal element into this article for one second), I know that it often happens that, when I have a large shovelful of coal in readiness for the fire, and the door to the fire box open as wide as it will go, there may be, nevertheless, the variation of perhaps an eighth of an inch between the point where the shovel should have ended the arc in its forward swing and the point at which it actually stops. In less technical phraseology, I sometimes tick the edge of the shovel against the threshold of the fire box, instead of shooting it over as should be done. Now, as I usually take a rather long, low swing, with considerable power behind it (if I do say so), the sudden contact of the shovel with the threshold re-

[67]

sults in a forceful projection of the many pieces of coal (and whatever else it is that comes with the coal for good measure) into all corners of the cellar. I have seen coal fly from my shovel under

"In less technical language, I sometimes tick the edge of the shovel against the threshold of the fire box."

such circumstances with such velocity as to land among the preserves at the other end of the cellar and in the opposite direction from which I was facing.

Now, this is obviously a waste of coal. It would be impossible to stoop all about the cellar picking up the vagrant pieces that had flown away, even if the blow of the shovel against the furnace had not temporarily paralyzed your hand and caused you to devote your entire attention to the coining of new and descriptive word pictures.

I would suggest, for this trouble, the taking of a " stance " in front of the fire box, with perhaps chalk markings for guidance of the feet at just the right distance away. Then a series of preparatory swings, as in driving off in golf, first with the empty shovel, then with a gradually increasing amount of coal. The only danger in this would be that you might bring the handle of the shovel back against an ash can or something behind you and thus spill about as much coal as before. But there, there—if you are going to borrow trouble like that, you might as well give up right now.

Another mishap of a somewhat similar nature occurs when a shovelful of ashes from under the grate is hit against the projecting shaker, causing the ashes to scatter over the floor and the shoes. This is a very discouraging thing to have happen, for, as the ashes are quite apt to contain at least three or four pieces of unburnt coal, it means that those pieces are as good as lost unless you have time to hunt them up. It also means shining the shoes again.

I find that an efficacious preventive for this is to take the shaker off when it is not in use and stand it in the corner. There the worst thing that it can do is to fall over against your shins when you are rummaging around for the furnace-bath-brush among the rest of the truck that hangs on the wall.

And, by the way, there are at least two pieces of long-handled equipment hanging on my cellar wall (items in the estate of the former tenant, who must have been a fancier of some sort) whose use I have never been able to figure out. I have tried them on various parts of the furnace at one time or another, but, as there is not much of anything that one on the outside of a furnace can do but *poke*, it seems rather silly to have half a dozen niblick-pokers and midiron-pokers with which to do it. One of these, resembling in shape a bridge, such as is used on all occasions by novices at pool, I experimented with one night and got it so tightly caught in back of the grate somewhere that I had to let the fire go out and take the dead coals out, piece by piece, through the door in order to get at the captive instrument and release it. And, of course, all this experimenting wasted coal.

The shaker is, however, an important factor in keeping the furnace going, for it is practically the only recourse in dislodging clinkers which have become stuck in the grate—that is, unless you can kick the furnace hard enough to shake them down. I have, in moments when, I am afraid, I was not quite myself, kicked the furnace with considerable force, but I never could see that it had any effect on the clinker. This, however, is no sign that it can't be done. I would be the first one to wish a man well who did it.

But, ordinarily, the shaker is the accepted agent for teaching the clinker its place. And, in the fancy assorted coal in vogue this season (one-third coal, one-third slate, and one-third rock candy) clinkers are running the combustible matter a slightly better than even race. This problem is, therefore, one which must be faced.

I find that a great deal of satisfaction, if not tangible results, can be derived from personifying the furnace and the recalcitrant clinker, and endowing them with human attributes, such as fear, chagrin, and susceptibility to physical and mental pain. In this fanciful manner the thing can be talked to as if it were a person, in this way lending a zest to the proceedings which would be entirely lacking in a contest with an inanimate object.

Thus, when it is discovered that the grate is stuck, you can say, *sotto voce:*

" Ho, ho! you * * * * * * * * * !   So that's your game, is it? "

[71]

(I would not attempt to dictate the particular epithets. Each man knows so much better than any one else just what gives him the most comfort in this respect that it would be presumptuous to lay down any formula. Personally, I have a wonderful set of remarks and proper names which I picked up one summer from a lobster man in Maine, which for soul-satisfying blasphemy are absolutely unbeatable. I will be glad to furnish this set to any one sending a stamped, self-addressed envelope.)

You then seize the shaker with both hands and give it a vicious yank, muttering between your teeth:

" We'll see, my fine fellow! We'll see! "

This is usually very effective in weakening the morale of the clinker, for it then realizes right at the start that it is pitted against a man who is not to be trifled with.

This should be followed by several short and powerful yanks, punctuated on the catch of each stroke with a muttered: " You * * * * * * * * * ! "

If you are short of wind, the force of this ejaculation may diminish as the yanks increase in number, in which case it will be well to rest for a few seconds.

At this point a little strategy may be brought

to bear. You can turn away, as if you were defeated, perhaps saying loudly, so that the clinker can hear: "Ho-hum! Well, I guess I'll call it a day," and pretend to start upstairs.

Then, quick as a wink, you should turn and leap back at the shaker, and, before the thing can recover from its surprise, give it a yank which will

"Quick as a wink you should turn and leap back at the shaker."

either rip it from its moorings or cause your own vertebræ to change places with a sharp click. It is a fifty-fifty chance.

But great caution should be observed before trying these heroic measures to make sure that the pins which hold the shaker in place are secure. A loosened pin will stand just so much shaking, and then it will unostentatiously work its way out and look around for something else to do. This always causes an awkward situation, for the yank next following the walkout of the pin, far from accomplishing its purpose of dispossessing the clinker, will precipitate you over backward among the ash cans with a viciousness in which it is impossible not to detect something personal.

Immediately following such a little upset to one's plans, it is perhaps the natural impulse to arise in somewhat of a pet and to set about exacting punitive indemnities. This does not pay in the end. If you hit any exposed portion of the furnace with the shaker the chances are that you will break it, which, while undoubtedly very painful to the furnace at the time, would eventually necessitate costly repairs. And, if you throw coal at it, you waste coal. This, if you remember, is an article on how to save coal.

Another helpful point is to prevent the fire from going out. This may be accomplished in one way that I am sure of. That is, by taking a book, or a ouija board, or some other indoor entertainment downstairs and sitting two feet away from the furnace all day, being relieved by your wife at night (or, needless to say, vice versa). I have never known this method of keeping the fire alive to fail, except when the watcher dropped off to sleep for ten or fifteen minutes. This is plenty of time for a raging fire to pass quietly away, and I can prove it.

Of course this treatment cuts in on your social life, but I know of nothing else that is infallible. I know of nothing else that can render impossible that depressing foreboding given expression by your wife when she says: " Have you looked at the fire lately? It's getting chilly here," followed by the apprehensive trip downstairs, eagerly listening for some signs of caloric life from within the asbestos-covered tomb; the fearful pause before opening the door, hoping against hope that the next move will disclose a ruddy glow which can easily be nursed back to health, but feeling, in the intuitive depths of your soul, that you might just as well begin crumpling up last Sunday's paper to ignite, for the Grim Reaper has passed this way.

And then the cautious pull at the door, opening it inch by inch, until the bitter truth is disclosed— a yawning cavern of blackness with the dull, gray outlines of consumed coals in the foreground, a dismal double-play: ashes to ashes.

These little thoughts on furnace tending and coal conservation are not meant to be taken as in any sense final. Some one else may have found the exact converse to be true; in which case he would do well to make a scientific account of it as I have done. It helps to buy coal.

VIII

NOT ACCORDING TO HOYLE

I HAVE just finished reading an article by an expert in auction bridge, and it has left me in a cold sweat. As near as I can make out, it presupposes that every one who plays bridge knows what he is doing before he does it, which simply means that I have been going along all this time working on exactly the wrong theory. It may incidentally explain why I have never been voted the most popular bridge player in Wimblehurst or presented with a loving cup by admiring members of the Neighborhood Club.

Diametrically opposed to the system of " think-before-you-play," advocated by this expert, my game has been built up purely on intuition. I rely almost entirely on the inner promptings of the moment in playing a card. I don't claim that there is anything spiritualistic about it, for it does not work out with consistent enough success to be in any way uncanny. As a matter of fact, it causes me a lot of trouble. When one relies on instinct to remind one of what the trumps are, or how many of them have been played, there is bound to be a slip-up every so often.

But what chagrins me, after reading the expert's article, is the thought that all this while I may have been playing with people who were actually thinking the thing out beforehand in a sordid sort of way, counting the trumps played and figuring on who had the queen or where the ten-spot lay. I didn't think there were such people in the world.

Here I have been going ahead, in an honest, hail-fellow-well-met mood, sometimes following suit, sometimes trumping my partner's trick, always taking it for granted that the idea was to get the hand played as quickly as possible in order to talk it over and tell each other how it might have been done differently.

It is true that, now and again, I have noticed sharp looks directed at me by my various partners, but I have usually attributed them to a little mannerism I have of humming softly while playing, and I have always stopped humming whenever my partner showed signs of displeasure, being perfectly willing to meet any one halfway in an effort to make the evening a pleasant one for all concerned. But now I am afraid that perhaps the humming was only a minor offense. I am appalled at the thought of what really was the trouble.

I should never have allowed myself to be dragged

into it at all. My first big mistake was made when, in a moment of weakness, I consented to learn the game; for a man who can frankly say "I do not play bridge" is allowed to go over in the corner

"Attributed them to a little mannerism I have of humming softly while playing."

and run the pianola by himself, while the poor neophyte, no matter how much he may protest that he isn't "at all a good player, in fact, I'm perfectly rotten," is never believed, but dragged into a game where it is discovered, too late, that he spoke the truth.

[79]

But it was a family affair at first. Dora belonged to a whist club which met every Friday afternoon on strictly partizan lines, except for once a year, when they asked the men in. My experience with this organization had been necessarily limited, as it held its sessions during my working hours. Once in a while, however, I would get home in time to meet in the front hall the stragglers who were just leaving, amid a general searching for furs and overshoes, and for some unaccountable reason I usually felt very foolish on such occasions. Certainly I had a right, under the Common Law, to be coming in my own front door, but I always had a sneaking feeling, there in the midst of the departing guests, that the laugh was on me.

One Friday, when I was confined to my room with a touch of neuralgia (it was in my face, if you are interested, and the whole right side swelled up until it was twice its normal size—I'd like to tell you more about it some time), I could hear the sounds of carnival going on downstairs. The noises made by women playing bridge are distinctive. At first the listener is aware of a sort of preliminary conversational murmur, with a running accompaniment of shuffling pasteboards. Then follows an unnatural quiet, punctuated by the thud of jeweled knuckles or the clank of bracelets as the cards are played

against the baize, with now and then little squeals
of dismay or delight from some of the more demon-
strative and an occasional " Good for you, partner! "
from an appreciative dummy. Gradually, as the
hand draws toward its close, there begins a low
sound, like the murmurings of the stage mob in
the wings, which rapidly increases, until the room
is filled with a shrill chatter, resembling that in the
Bird House in Central Park, from which there is
distinguishable merely a wild medley:

" If you had led me your queen—was so afraid
she might trump in with—my dear, I didn't have a
face card in my—threw away just the wrong—had
the jack, 10, 9, and 7—thought Alice had the
king—ace and three little ones—how about honors?
—my dear, *simply* frightful—if you had returned my
lead—my *dear!* "

This listening in at bridge, however, was the nearest I had ever been to the front, until it came time
for the Friday Afternoon Club to let down the bars
and have a Men's Night. I had no illusions about
this " Men's Night," but it was a case of my learning to play bridge and accompanying Dora, or of
her getting some man in from off the sidewalk to
take my place, and I figured that it would cause less
talk if I were there to play myself. As I think it
over now, I feel that the strange-man scheme might

have worked out with less comment being made than my playing drew down.

But it was for this purpose that I allowed myself to be instructed in the rudiments of bridge. I had nothing permanent in mind in absorbing these principles, fully expecting to forget them again the day after the party. I miscalculated by about one day, it now seems.

The expert, whose article has been such an inspiration to me, had some neat little diagrams drawn for him, showing just where the cards lay in the four hands, and with the players indicated as A, B, Y, and Z; apparently the same people, come up in the world, who, in our algebras some years ago, used to buy and sell apples to each other with feverish commercialism and to run races with all sorts of unfair handicaps. What a small world it is, after all!

It seems to me, therefore, that, since this is a pretty fairly technical article, it might be well if I were to utilize the same diagrammatic device and terse method of description, to show the exact course of the first hand in which I participated at the party.

A and B are our opponents, X my partner, and I (oddly enough) myself. A is Ralph Thibbets, one of those cool devils who think they know all about a game, and usually do. He has an irritating way of laying down his cards, when the hand is about half played, and saying: "Well, the rest are mine," and the most irritating part of it all is that, when you have insisted on figuring it out for yourself, he is found to be right. I disliked him from the first.

B is Mrs. Lucas, who breathes hard and says nothing, but clanks her cards down with finality, seeming to say: "That for you!" She got me nervous.

X, my partner, used to be a good friend of mine. And, so far as I am concerned, I would be perfectly willing to let bygones be bygones and be on friendly terms again.

In utilizing the expert's method of description, I shall improve on it slightly by also indicating the conversation accompanying each play, a feature which is of considerable importance in a game.

B deals, and finally makes it three diamonds, after X has tried to bid hearts without encouragement from me. I pass as a matter of principle, not being at all sure of this bidding proposition.

I lead, with a clear field and no particular object in view, the 8 of diamonds. It looks as uncompromising as any card in my hand. "Leading *trumps!*" says X with a raising of the eyebrows. "What do you know about that!" I exclaim. "I had forgotten that they were trumps. I must be asleep. Like the old Irishman when St. Peter asked him where he came from, and he said: ' Begorra—' " A cuts this story short by playing the 3 of diamonds; X, with some asperity, discards the 3 of spades, and B takes the trick with the 10-spot. Silence.

" That story of the Irishman and St. Peter," I continue, " was told to me by a fellow in Buffalo last week who had just come from France. He said that while he was in a place called ' Mousong,' or ' Mousang,' he actually saw—"

" Your play," says X. " Oh, I beg your pardon," I say, " whose jack of spades is that? " " Mine," says B, drumming on the table with her finger nails and looking about the room at the pictures. Having more poor diamonds than anything else in my hand, and aiming to get them out of the way as soon as possible to give the good cards a chance, I play the 5 of diamonds.

" What, trumping it? Have you no spades? " shouts A. I can see that I have him rattled; so, although, as a matter of fact, I have got plenty of spades, I smile knowingly and sit tight. These smart Alecs make me sick, telling me what I should play and what I should not play. A accepts the inevitable and plays his 2-spot. X, considerably cheered up, plays the 4 and says: " Our trick, partner." I pick up the cards and mix them with those already in my hand, reverting, for the time, to poker tactics. This error, alone among all that I make during the game, is unobserved.

"Well, I suppose that you people are all excited over that new baby up at your house," I say pleasantly to A, just to show him that I can be gracious in victory as well as in defeat. "Let's see, is it a boy or a girl? "

" It's *your lead!* " he replies shortly.

" I beg your pardon," I say; " I certainly must be asleep to-night." And, as my thumb is on the 5 of diamonds, I lead it.

"Here, here! " says A, "wasn't it the 5 of diamonds that you trumped in with just a minute ago? " That man has second-sight. As a matter of fact, I suspect that there is something crooked about him. " Yes, it is," corroborates B in her longest speech of the evening. X says: " Where *is* that trick that we took? " And then it is discovered that it has found its way into my hand, from which it is disentangled with considerable trouble and segregated. As for me, I pass the whole thing off as a joke.

" I saw in the paper this morning," I began when the situation has become a little less complicated, " where a woman in Perth Amboy found a

"'Here, here!' says A, 'wasn't it the 5 of diamonds you trumped in with a minute ago?'"

hundred dollars in the lining of an old lounge in—"

"It's your lead, if you don't mind," says A very distinctly. "You have made only one false start out of a possible three. Try again." I pretend not to hear this sarcasm, and, just to show him that there is life in the old dog yet, I lead my ace of spades.

"Look here, my dear sir!" says A, quite upset by now. "Only one hand ago you refused spades and trumped them. That revoking on your part gives us three tricks and we throw up the hand."

"Fair enough," I retort cheerfully, "three is just what you bid, isn't it? Quite a coincidence, I call it," and with that I throw my cards on the table with considerable relief. Nothing good could have come of this hand, even if we had played until midnight.

From all sides now arose the familiar sounds of the post-mortem: "I had the jack, 10, 9, and 7, all good, but I just couldn't get in with them. . . . If you had only led me your king, we could have set them at least two. . . . I knew that Grace had the queen, but I didn't dare try to finesse. . . . We had simple honors. . . . As soon as I saw you leading spades, I knew that there was nothing in it," etc., etc.

But at our table there was no post-mortem. Not

because there had been no death, but there seemed to be nothing to say about it. So we sat, marking down our scores, until Dora came up behind me and said: " Well, dear, how is your game coming on? "

As no one else seemed about to speak, I said: " Oh, finely, I'm getting the hang of it in no time."

My partner muttered something about hanging being too good, which seemed a bit uncalled for.

And so I went through the evening, meeting new people and making new friends. And, owing to Dora's having neglected to teach me the details of score keeping, I had to make a system up for myself, with the result that I finished the evening with a total of 15,000 points on my card and won the first prize.

" Beginner's luck," I called it with modest good nature.

IX

FROM NINE TO FIVE

ONE of the necessary qualifications of an efficient business man in these days of industrial literature seems to be the ability to write, in clear and idiomatic English, a 1,000-word story on how efficient he is and how he got that way. A glance through any one of our more racy commercial magazines will serve nicely to illustrate my point, for it was after glancing through one of them only five minutes ago that the point suggested itself to me.

"What Is Making Our Business Grow; " "My $10,000 System of Carbon-Copy Hunting; " "Making the Turn-Over Turn In; " "If I Can Make My Pencil Sharpenings Work, Why Can't You? " "Getting Sales Out of Sahara," etc., are some of the intriguing titles which catch the eye of the student of world affairs as he thumbs over the business magazines on the news-stands before buying his newspaper. It seems as if the entire business world were devoting its working hours to the creation of a school of introspective literature.

[89]

But the trouble with these writers is that they are all successful. There is too much sameness to their stuff. They have their little troubles at first, it is true, such as lack of coördination in the central typing department, or congestion of office boys in the room where the water cooler is situated; but sooner or later you may be perfectly sure that Right will triumph and that the young salesman will bring in the order that puts the firm back on its feet again. They seem to have no imagination, these writers of business confessions. What the art needs is some Strindberg of Commerce to put down on paper the sordid facts of Life as they really are, and to show, in bitter words of cynical realism, that ink erasers are not always segregated or vouchers always all that they should be, and that, behind the happy exterior of many a mahogany railing, all is not so gosh-darned right with the world after all.

Now, without setting myself up as a Strindberg, I would like to start the ball rolling toward a more realistic school of business literature by setting down in my rough, impulsive way a few of the items in the account of " How We Make Our Business Lose $100,000 a Year."

All that I ask in the way of equipment is an illustration showing a square-jawed, clean-cut American business man sitting at a desk and shaking his finger at another man, very obviously the head of the sales department because it says so under the picture, who is standing with his thumbs in the arm-

"A square-jawed American business man, etc., shaking his finger at another."

holes of his waistcoat, gnawing at a big, black cigar, and looking out through the window at the smoke-stacks of the works. With this picture as a starter, and a chart or two, I can build up a very decent business story around them.

In the first place let me say that what we have done in our business any firm can do in theirs. It is not that we have any extraordinary talents along organization lines. We simply have taken the lessons learned in everyday trading, have tabulated and filed them in triplicate. Then we have forgotten them.

I can best give an idea of the secret of our mediocrity as a business organization by outlining a typical day in our offices. I do this in no spirit of boasting, but simply to show these thousands of systematized business men who are devoting themselves to literature that somewhere in all this miasma of success there shines a ray of inefficiency, giving promise of the day that is to come.

The first part of the morning in our establishment is devoted to the mail. This starts the day off right, for it gives every one something to do, which is, I have found, a big factor in keeping the place looking busy.

Personally I am not what is known as a " snappy " dictator. It makes me nervous to have a stenographer sitting there waiting for me to say something so that she can pounce on it and tear it into hieroglyphics. I feel that, mentally, she is checking me up with other men who have dictated to her, and that I am being placed in Class 5a, along with the licensed pilots and mental defectives, and the more I think of it the more incoherent I become. If exact and detailed notes were to be preserved of one of my dictated letters, mental processes, and all, they might read something like this:

" Good morning, Miss Kettle. . . . Take a letter, please . . . to the Nipco Drop Forge and Tool Company, Schenectady . . . S-c-h-e-c — er — well, Schenectady; you know how to spell that, I guess, Miss Kettle, ha! ha! . . . Nipco Drop Forge and Tool Company, Schenectady, New York. . . . Gentlemen—er (business of touching finger tips and looking at the ceiling meditatively)—Your favor of the 17th inst. at hand, and in reply would state that —er (I should have thought this letter out before beginning to dictate and decided just what it *is* that we desire to state in reply)—and in reply would state that—er . . . our Mr. Mellish reports that— er . . . where is that letter from Mr. Mellish, Miss Kettle? . . . The one about the castings. . . . Oh, never mind, I guess I can remember what he said. . . . Let's see, where were we? . . . Oh, yes, that our Mr. Mellish reports that he shaw the sipment— I mean *saw* the *shipment*—what's the matter with me? (this girl must think that I'm a perfect fool) . . . that he shaw the sipment in question on the platform of the station at Miller's Falls, and that it —er . . . ah . . . ooom . . . (I'll have this girl asleep in her chair in a minute. I'll bet that she goes and tells the other girls that she has just taken a

[93]

letter from a man with the mind of an eight-year-old boy). . . . We could, therefore, comma, . . . what's the matter? . . . Oh, I didn't finish that other sentence, I guess. . . . Let's see, how did it go? . . . Oh, yes . . . and that I, or rather *it*, was in good shape . . . er, cross that out, please (this girl is simply wasting her time here. I could spell this out with alphabet blocks quicker and let her copy it) . . . and that it was in excellent shape at that shape—er . . . or rather, at that *time* . . . er . . . period. New paragraph.

"We are, comma, therefore, comma, unable to . . . hello, Mr. Watterly, be right with you in half a second. . . . I'll finish this later, Miss Kettle . . . thank you."

When the mail is disposed of we have what is known as Memorandum Hour. During this period every one sends memoranda to every one else. If you happen to have nothing in particular about which to dictate a memorandum, you dictate a memorandum to some one, saying that you have nothing to suggest or report. This gives a stimulating exchange of ideas, and also helps to use up the blue memorandum blanks which have been printed at some expense for just that purpose.

As an example of how this system works, I will give a typical instance of its procedure. My partner, let us say, comes in and sits down at the desk opposite me. I observe that his scarfpin is working its way out from his tie. I call a stenographer and say: " Take a memo to Mr. MacFurdle, please. *In re* Loosened Scarfpin. You are losing your scarfpin."

As soon as she has typed this it is given to Mr. MacFurdle's secretary, and a carbon copy is put in the files. Mr. MacFurdle, on receiving my memo, adjusts his scarfpin and calls his secretary.

" A memo to Mr. Benchley, please. *In re* Tightened Scarfpin. Thank you. I have given the matter my attention."

As soon as I have received a copy of this typewritten reply to my memorandum we nod pleasantly to each other and go on with our work. In all, not more than half an hour has been consumed, and we have a complete record of the negotiations in our files in case any question should ever arise concerning them. In case *no* question should ever arise, we still have the complete record. So we can't lose—unless you want to call that half hour a loss.

It is then almost lunch time. A quick glance at a pile of carbons of mill reports which have but little significance to me owing to the fact that the figures are illegible (it being a fifth-string carbon);

a rapid survey of the matter submitted for my O. K., most of which I dislike to take the responsibility for and therefore pass on to Mr. Houghtelling for his O. K.; a short tussle in the washroom with the liquid-soap container which contains no liquid soap and a thorough drying of the hands on my handkerchief, the paper towels having given out early in the morning, and I am ready to go to lunch with a man from the Eureka Novelty Company who wants to sell us a central paste-supply system (whereby all the office paste is kept in one large vat in the storeroom, individual brushfuls being taken out only on requisitions O. K.'d by the head of the department).

Both being practical business men, we spend only two hours at lunch. And, both being practical business men, we know all the subtleties of selling. It is a well-known fact that personality plays a big rôle in the so-called " selling game " (one of a series of American games, among which are " the newspaper game," " the advertising game," " the cloak-and-suit game," " the ladies' mackintosh and over-shoe game," " the seedless-raisin and dried-fruit game," etc.), and so Mr. Ganz of the Eureka Novelty Company spends the first hour and three-quarters developing his " personality appeal." All through the tomato bisque aux croutons and the roast prime ribs of beef, dish gravy, he puts into practice the principles enunciated in books on Selling, by means of which the subject at hand is deferred in a subtle manner until the salesman has had a chance to impress his prospect with his geniality and his smile (an attractive smile has been known to sell a carload of 1897 style derbies, according to authorities on The Smile in Selling), his knowledge of baseball, his rich fund of stories, and his general aversion to getting down to the disagreeable reason for his call.

The only trouble with this system is that I have done the same thing myself so many times that I know just what his next line is going to be, and can figure out pretty accurately at each stage of his conversation just when he is going to shift to one position nearer the thing he has to sell. I know that he has not the slightest interest in my entertainment other than the sale of a Eureka Central Paste Supply System, and he knows that I know it, and so we spend an hour and three-quarters fooling the waiter into thinking that we are engaged in disinterested camaraderie.

For fifteen minutes we talk business, and I agree to take the matter up with the directors at the next meeting, holding the mental reservation that a central paste supply system will be installed in our plant only over my dead body.

OF ALL THINGS!

This takes us until two-thirty, and I have to hurry back to a conference. We have two kinds of "conference." One is that to which the office boy refers when he tells the applicant for a job that Mr. Blevitch is "in conference." This means that Mr. Blevitch is in good health and reading the paper, but otherwise unoccupied. The other kind of "conference" is bona fide in so far as it implies that three or four men are talking together in one room, and don't want to be disturbed.

This conference is on, let us say, the subject of Window Cards for display advertising: shall they be triangular or diamond-shaped?

There are four of us present, and we all begin by biting off the ends of four cigars. Watterly has a pile of samples of window cards of various shapes, which he hangs, with a great deal of trouble, on the wall, and which are not referred to again. He also has a few ideas on Window Card Psychology.

" It seems to me," he leads off, " that we have here a very important question. On it may depend the success of our Middle Western sales. The problem as I see it is this: what will be the reaction on the retina of the eye of a prospective customer made by the sight of a diamond-shaped card hanging in a window? It is a well-known fact in applied psychology that when you take the average man into a darkened room, loosen his collar, and shout "Diamonds! " at him suddenly, his mental reaction is one in which the ideas of Wealth, Value, Richness, etc.,

" The problem as I see it is this."

predominate. Now, it stands to reason that the visual reaction from seeing a diamond-shaped card in the window will . . ."

" Excuse me a moment, George," says MacFurdle, who has absorbed some pointers on Distribution from a book entitled " The World Salesman," " I don't think that it is so important to get after the psychology of the thing first as it is to outline thoroughly the Theory of Zone Apportionment on which we are going to work. If we could make up a chart, showing in red ink the types of retail-stores and in green ink the types of jobber establishments, in this district, then we could get at the window display from that angle and tackle the psychology later, if at all. Now, on such a chart I would try to show the zones of Purchasing Power, and from these could be deduced . . ."

"Just a minute, Harry," Inglesby interrupts, "let me butt in for half a second. That chart system is all very well when you are selling goods with which the public is already familiar through association with other brands, but with ours it is different. We have got to estimate the Consumer Demand first in terms of dollar-and-a-quarter units, and build our selling organization up around that. Now, if I know anything about human nature at all—and I think I do, after being in the malleable-iron game for fifteen years—the people in this section of the country represent an entirely different trade current than . . ."

At this point I offer a few remarks on one of my pet hobbies, the influence of the Gulf Stream on Regional Commerce, and then we all say again the same things that we said before, after which we say them again, the pitch of the conversation growing higher at each repetition of views and the room becoming more and more filled with cigar smoke.

FROM NINE TO FIVE

Our final decision is to have a conference to-morrow afternoon, before which each one is to " think the matter over and report his reactions."

This brings the day to a close. There has been nothing remarkable in it, as the reader will be the first one to admit. And yet it shows the secret of whatever we have not accomplished in the past year in our business.

And it also shows why we practical business men have so little sympathy with a visionary, impractical arrangement like this League of Nations. President Wilson was all right in his way, but he was too academic. What we practical men in America want is deeds, not words.

X

TURNING OVER A NEW LEDGER LEAF

NEW YEAR'S morning approximately ninety-two million people in these United States will make another stab at keeping personal and household accounts for the coming year.

One month from New Year's there will be approximately seventy-three of these accountants still in the race (all started). Of these, sixty will be groggy but still game and willing to lump the difference between the actual balance in their pockets and the theoretical balance in the books under the elastic heading " General Expenses " or " Incidentals," and start again for February. The remaining thirteen, who came out even, will be either professors of accounting in business schools or out and out unreliable.

This high mortality rate among amateur accountants is one of the big problems of modern household efficiency, and is exceeded in magnitude only by the number of schemes devised to simplify household accounting. Every domestic magazine, in the midst of its autobiographical accounts of unhappy marriages, must needs run a chart showing how far a family with an income of $1,500 a year can go without getting caught and still put something aside for a canary. Every insurance company has had prepared by experts a table of figures explaining how, by lumping everything except Rent and Incidentals under Luxuries and doing without them, you can save enough from the wreckage of $1,200 a year to get in on their special Forty-Year Adjournment Policy.

Those publications which cannot get an expert to figure out how much you ought to spend per egg per hen-day will publish letters from young housewives showing how they made out a budget which in the end brought them in more money than they earned and had the grocer and electric light company owing them money.

The trouble with all these vicarious budgets is that they presuppose, on the part of the user, an ability to add and subtract. They take it for granted that you are going to do the thing right. Now, with all due respect to our primary and secondary school system, this is absurd. Here and there you may find some one who can take a page of figures and maul them over so that they will come out right at the bottom, but who wants to be a man like that? What fun does he get out of life, always sure of what the result is going to be?

As for me, give me the regular method of addition by logic; that is, if the result obtained is twelve removed from the result that should have been obtained, then, ergo, twelve is the amount by which you have miscalculated and it should, therefore, be added or subtracted, as the case may be, to or from the actual result somewhere up in the middle of the column, so that in the end the thing will balance. And there you are, with just the same result as if you had worked for hours over the page and quibbled over every little point and figure. There is no sense in becoming a slave to numerical signs which in themselves are not worth the paper they are written on. It is the imagination that one puts into accounting that makes it fascinating. If free verse, why not free arithmetic?

It is for the honest ones, who admit that they can't work one of the budget systems for the mentally alert, that the accompanying one has been devised.

Let us take, for instance, a family whose income is $750,000 a year, exclusive of tips. In the family are a father, mother and fox terrier. The expenses for such a family come under the head of Liabilities and are distributed among six accounts:

TURNING OVER A NEW LEAF

Food, Lodging, Extras, Extras, Incidentals and Extras. For this couple I would advise the following system:

Take the contents of the weekly pay envelope, $14,423.08 (if any one is mean enough to go and divide $750,000 into fifty-two parts to see if I have got it right, he will find that it doesn't quite come to eight cents, but you certainly wouldn't have me carry it out to any more places. It took me from three yesterday afternoon until after dinner to do what I did). Take the contents of the envelope and lay them on the kitchen table in little piles, so much for meat, so much for eggs, so much for adhesive plaster, etc., until the kitchen table is covered. Then sweep it all into a bag and balance your books.

Balancing the books is another point in the ideal system which often makes for trouble. Sticklers for form insist that the two sides of the page shall come out alike, even at the expense of your self-respect. It is the artificiality of this that hurts. No matter how much you spend, no matter how much you receive, at the bottom of the page they must add up to the same thing, with a double red line underneath them to show that the polls are closed.

But since this is the accepted way of doing the thing, we might just as well concede the point and lay our plans accordingly. First take the sum that you have left over in the household exchequer at the end of the mouth. Put it, or its equivalent in check form, on the table in front of you. Then, working backward, find out how much you have spent since the first of the month. This sum is the crux of the whole system. Divide it into as many equal parts as you have accounts. For instance, Food, Rent, Clothes, Insurance and Savings, Operating Expenses, Higher Life. If you can't divide it so that it comes out even, tuck a little bit on the Higher Life account. And, as the student of French says, " *Voilà* " (there it is)!

Perhaps you have wondered what I meant by " Higher Life." I have. It might be well to state it here so that we can all get it clear in our minds. Under the " Higher Life " account you can charge everything that you want to do, but feel that you can't afford. If you want to take in an inconsequential theatrical performance and can't quite square it with your conscience, figure it out this way: By going to that show you will become so disgusted with the futility of such things that you will come out of the theater all aglow with a resolve to do a man's work in the world just as soon as you have caught up with your sleep. Surely that comes under " Advancement " or " Higher Life."

TURNING OVER A NEW LEAF

Insurance budget helps always include under "Advancement" money spent for lectures. Now, it may be that I have drifted away from the big things in life since I moved out into the country, but somehow I can't just at this moment recollect standing in line at a box office for a lecture. But then, my home life is very pleasant.

Lectures would be a very convenient heading, nevertheless, to have in your budget. Then, any little items that slip your attention during the month you can group under lectures and mark off ten paces in your advancement chart.

By way of outlining beforehand just what you can spend on this and that (and it is usually on "that") it might be well to take another family with a representative income. Let us say that there are four in the family and that the income is about $1,000 per year too small. If such a family would sit down some evening and draw a chart showing father's earning capacity with one red line and the family spending capacity with one black line, they would not only have a pleasant evening, but they would have a nice, neat chart all drawn and suitable for framing.

There is one little technical point that the amateur accountant will do well to remember. It gives a distinction to the page and shows that you are acquainted with bookkeeping lore. It is this: Label your debit column " credits " and your credit column " debits." You might think that what you receive into the exchequer would be credited and

" They would have a nice, neat chart suitable for framing."

your expenses debited, but that is where you miss the whole theory of practical accounting. That would be too simple to be efficient. You must wax transcendental, and say, " I, as an individuated entity, am nothing. Everything is all; all is everything." There is a transcendent Account, to which all other accounts are responsible, and hence money turned over to the Cinnamon Account is not credited to that account, but rather debited to it, for Cinnamon hereby assumes the responsibility for the sum. As money is spent for Cinnamon, its account is credited, for it is relieved of that responsibility. Don't start wondering where the responsibility finally settles or you will throw something out of its stride in your brain.

Some people profess to scoff at the introduction of bookkeeping into the running of the household. It is simply because they never tasted the fascination of the thing.

The advantage of keeping family accounts is clear. If you do not keep them you are uneasily aware of the fact that you are spending more than you are earning. If you do keep them, you *know* it.

A PIECE OF ROAST BEEF

PERSONALLY, I class roast beef with water-cress and vanilla cornstarch pudding as tasty articles of diet. It undoubtedly has more than the required number of calories; it leans over backward in its eagerness to stand high among our best proteins, and, according to a vivid chart in the back of the cookbook, it is equal in food value to three dried raisins piled one on the other plus peanut-butter the size of an egg.

But for all that I can't seem to feel that I am having a good time while I am eating it. It stimulates the same nerve centers in me that a lantern-slide lecture on " Palestine—the Old and the New," does.

However, I have noticed that there are people who are not bored by it; in fact, I have seen them deliberately order it in a restaurant when they had the choice of something else; so I thought that the only fair thing I could do would be to look into the matter and see if, in this great city, there weren't

A PIECE OF ROAST BEEF

some different ways of serving roast beef to vary its monotony.

Roast beef is not the same price in all eating-places. What makes the difference? What does a diner at the Ritz get in his " roast prime ribs of beef au jus " that makes it distinctive from the " Special to-day—roast beef and mashed potatoes " of the Bowery restaurant?

To answer these questions I started out on a tour of the representative eating-places of some of our best known strata of society, and, whatever my conclusions are, you may be sure that they are thoroughly inexpert.

First, I tried out what is known as the Bay State Lunch, so called because on Thursdays they have a fishcake special. It is one of the hundreds of " self-serving " lunchrooms, where you approach the marble counter and give your order in a low tone to a man in a barber's coat, and then repeat it at intervals of one minute, each time louder and each time to a different man, until you are forced to point to a tub of salmon salad and say, " Some of that," for which your ticket is punched and you are allowed to take your portion and nurse it on the over-developed arm of a chair.

Here the roast beef shot through the Punch and Judy arrangement in the wall, a piece of meat about as large around as a man's-size mitten, steeping in its own gravy and of a pale reddish hue. The price was twenty cents, which included a dab of mashed potato dished out in an ice-cream scoop, a generous allowance of tender peas, two hot tea-biscuits and butter to match.

"Considering the basic ingredient it was a perfectly satisfactory meal."

Considering the basic ingredient, it was a perfectly satisfactory meal, and I felt that twenty cents was little enough to pay for it, especially since it was going in on my expense account.

For the next experiment I went to a restaurant where business men are wont to gather for luncheon, men who pride themselves on their acumen and adherence to the principles of efficiency. The place

A PIECE OF ROAST BEEF

has a French name and its menus are printed on a card the size of a life insurance company's complimentary calendar, always an ominous sign. The roast beef here was served cold, with a plate of escarole salad (when I was a boy I used to have to dig escarole out of the front lawn with a trowel so that the grass could have a chance) for seventy-five cents.

The meat bulked a little larger than at the Bay State Lunch, but when the fat had been cut away and trimmed off the salvage was about the size of a boy's mitten. As for the taste, the only difference that I could detect was that one had been hot and the other cold.

And, incidentally, the waiter had some bosom friends in the next room who fascinated him so that it was all I could do to make him see that if he didn't come around to me once in a while, just as a matter of form, there would be no way for me to tip him. Beef and salad, plus tip, ninety cents.

That evening I ambled up the Bowery until I came to the Busy Home Restaurant. On a blackboard in front was written, " Roast Beef, Mashed Potatoes and Coffee, 10 Cents." My old hunger again seized me. I said to myself: " Look here! Be a man! This thing is getting the best of you." But before I knew it I was inside and seated at an oilcloth-covered table, saying, in a hoarse voice, " Roast beef! "

The waiter was dressed in an informal costume, with his shirt-sleeves rolled up and a mulatto apron about his waist, but he smiled genially when he took my order and was back with it in two minutes. The article itself was of the regulation size, cut somewhat thinner, perhaps, and bordering on the gray in hue, but undoubtedly roast beef. It, too, had an affinity for its own gravy and hid itself modestly under an avalanche of mashed potatoes. A cup of coffee was also included in the ten cents' initial expense, but I somehow wasn't coffee-thirsty that night, and so didn't sample it. But I did help myself to the plate piled high with fresh bread which was left in front of me. All in all, it was what I should call a representative roast beef dinner. And I got more than ten cents' worth of calories, I know.

But so far I had kept below the Fourteenth Street belt in my investigations. Roast beef is a cosmopolitan habit, and knows no arbitrary boundaries; so I went uptown. Into one of the larger of our largest hotels, one which is not so near the Grand Central Station as to be in the train-shed, and yet not so far removed from it as to be represented by a different Assemblyman. Here, I felt, would be the test. Could roast beef come back? Surrounded

A PIECE OF ROAST BEEF

by glittering chandeliers and rich tapestries, snowy table linen and silver service, here was the chance for the ordinary roast beef to become a veritable dainty, with some character, some distinctive touch that should lift it above all that roast beef has ever meant before. I entered the dining-room, in high hopes.

Clad in a walking suit of virile tweed, I considered myself respectably dressed. Not ostentatiously respectable, mind you, but, since most of the other diners were in evening dress, rather *distingué*, I thought.

But apparently the hotel retainers weren't trained to look through a rough exterior and find the sterling qualities beneath. They looked through my rough exterior all right, but they didn't stop at my sterling qualities. They looked right through to the man behind me, and gave him the signal that there was a seat for him.

Not to be outdone, however, I got my place in the sun by cleverly tripping my rival as he passed me, so that he fell into the fountain arrangement, while I sat down in the seat pulled out for him by the head waiter. And, once I was in, there was nothing for them to do but let me stay.

After I had been there a few minutes a waiter came and put on a fresh table cloth. Five minutes later another man placed a knife and spoon at my plate. Later in the evening a boy with a basket of rolls wandered by and deposited one on my table with a pair of pincers. Personally, I was rather glad that it was working out this way, for it would make my story all the better, but I might have really been in a hurry for my dinner.

It wasn't long, as the crow flies, before one of the third assistant waiters unloosened enough to drop round and see if there was anything else I wanted besides one roll and a knife and spoon. I looked over the menu as if I were in a pretty captious mood, and then, with the air of an epicure who has tasted to the dregs all the condiments of Arabia and whose jaded palate refuses to thrill any longer, I ordered " roast beef."

It was billed as " 90 (.80)," which didn't strike me as being very steep, considering the overhead expense there must be in keeping little knots of waiters and 'bus-boys standing round doing nothing in the further corner of the room.

The waiter wasn't very enthusiastic over my order, and something saved me from asking him if they threw in " a side " of mashed potatoes with the meat. He seemed to expect something more, even after I had ordered potatoes, so I suggested an artichoke. That cheered him up more than any-

A PIECE OF ROAST BEEF

"The waiter wasn't very enthusiastic over my order."

thing I had done that evening, and he really got quite fratty and said: " A little salad, sir? " Again I imitated a man who has had more experience with salads than any other three men put together and who has found them a miserable sham.

" No; that will be all for now," I said, and turned wearily away. I wanted to tell him that I had a dinner coat at home that looked enough sight better than his, but there is no use in making a scene when it can be avoided.

During the next twenty minutes the orchestra played once and I ate my roll. Then the roast beef came.

On a silver platter, with a silver cover, it was placed before me under the best possible scenic conditions. But the thing that met my gaze when the cover was lifted might just as well have been the same property piece of roast beef that was keeping company with a dab of mashed potato in the Bay State Lunch. It had a trifle more fat, was just a shade pinker, and perhaps a micrometer could have detected a bit more bulk; but, so far as I was concerned or so far as the calories were concerned, it was the same. I won't say that it was the same as the Roast Beef Special of the Bowery Restaurant, because the service in the Bowery Restaurant was infinitely better.

A PIECE OF ROAST BEEF

As a fitting garniture to such a dish, there was a corsage of watercress draped on the corner of the salver. At any rate, it could be said for it that it was not intoxicating, and so could never cause any real misery in this world.

I nibbled at my roast beef, but my spirit was broken. I had gone through a week of self-denial, ordering roast beef when I craved edibles, eating at restaurants while my family waited for me at home, and here was the result of my researches: Roast beef is roast beef, and nothing can prevent it. From the ten-cent order of the Busy Home Restaurant, up through to the piece I was then eating, it was the same grim reality, the only justification for a difference in price being a silver salver or a waiter in a tuxedo.

"But," I said to myself, "eighty cents isn't so much, at that. Besides, I have heard the orchestra play one tune every half-hour, and have had a kind word from one of the *chargés d'affaires* of the waiter's staff."

This quite reconciled me, until my check was brought. There, added to the initial expense of eighty cents, was the upkeep, such as "Cover, 25c." "Potatoes, 30c." And to this must be added the modest fee of twenty cents to the waiter and ten cents to the hat-boy who gave me the wrong hat.

[119]

OF ALL THINGS!

Total expense for one piece of roast beef, $1.70.

These investigations may not prove to be much of a contribution to modern science or economics. I doubt if they are ever incorporated in any textbook, even if it should be a textbook on this very subject. But I must take credit to myself for one thing: Not once throughout the whole report have I alluded to the Tenderloin District.

XII

THE COMMUNITY MASQUE AS A
SUBSTITUTE FOR WAR

WITH War and Licker removed from the list of "What's Going on This Week," how will mankind spend the long summer evenings? Some advocate another war. Others recommend a piece of yeast in a glass of grape-juice. The effect is said to be equally devastating.

But there is a new school, led by Percy Mackaye, which brings forward a scheme for occupying the spare time of the world which has, at least, the savor of novelty. It presents the community masque as a substitute for war. Whenever a neighborhood, or county, feels the old craving for blood-letting and gas-bombing coming on, a town meeting is to be called and plans drawn up for the presentation of a masque entitled "Democracy" or "From Chrysalis to Butterfly." In this simple way, one and all will be kept out in the open air and will get to know each other better, thus relieving their bellicose cravings right there on the village green among themselves, without dragging a foreign na-

tion into the mess at all. The slogan is " Fight
Your Neighbors First. Why Go Abroad for War? "

The community masque idea is all right in itself.
There certainly can be no harm in dressing up to
represent the Three Platoon System, or the Spirit
of Machinery, and reciting free verse to the effect
that:

" I am the Three Platoon System. Firemen I rep-
   resent,
   And the clash and clang of the Hook and Ladder
   Company."

No one could find fault with that, provided that
those taking part in the thing do so of their own
free will and understand what they are doing.

The trouble with the community masque is not
so much with the masque as with the community.
For while the masque may be a five star sporting
extra hot from the presses of Percy Mackaye, the
community is the same old community that has
been getting together for inter-Sunday School track-
meets and Wig and Footlight Club Amateur The-
atricals for years and years, and the result has always been the same.

Let us say, for instance, that the community of
Wimblehurst begins to feel the lack of a good, rous-

ing war to keep the Ladies' Guild and the men over thirty-five busy. What could be more natural than to call in Mr. Mackaye, and say: " What have you got in the way of a nice masque for a suburban district containing many socially possible people and others who might do very well in ensemble work? "

Something entitled " The March of Civilization " is selected, because it calls for Boy Scout uniforms and a Goddess of Liberty costume, all of which are on hand, together with lots of Red Cross regalia, left over from the war drives. The plot of the thing concerns the adventures of the young girl *Civilization* who leaves her home in the *Neolithic Period* accompanied only by her faithful old nurse *Language* and *Language's* little children the *Vowels* and the *Consonants*. She is followed all the way from the *Neolithic Age* to the Present Time by the evil spirit, *Indigestion*, but, thanks to the helpful offices of the *Spirits of Capillary Attraction*, and *Indestructibility of Matter*, she overcomes all obstacles and reaches her goal, *The League of Nations*, at last.

But during the course of her wanderings, there have been all kinds of sub-plots which bring the element of suspense into the thing. For instance, it seems that this person *Indigestion* has found out

something about *Civilization's* father which gives
him the upper hand over the girl, and he, together
with the two gunmen, *Heat* and *Humidity,* arrange
all kinds of traps for the poor thing to fall into.
But she takes counsel with the kind old lady, *Self-
Determination of Peoples*, and is considerably
helped by the low comedy character, *Obesity,* who
always appears at just the right moment. So in the
end, there is a big ensemble, involving Boy Scouts,
representatives of those Allies who happen to be in
good standing in that particular month, seven boys
and girls personifying the twelve months of the year,
Red Cross workers, the Mayor's Committee of Wel-
come, a selection of Major Prophets, children typi-
fying the ten different ways of cooking an egg, and
the all-pervading *Spirit of the Post-Office Department,* seated on a daïs in the rear and watching over
the assemblage with kindly eyes and an armful of
bricks.

This, then, is in brief outline, " The March of
Civilization," selected for presentation by the Community Council of Wimblehurst. It is to be done
on the edge of the woods which line the golf-
course, and on paper, the thing shapes up rather
well.

Considerable hard feeling arises, however, over
the choice of the children to play the parts of the

Vowels and the *Consonants*. It is, of course, not possible to have all the vowels and consonants represented, as they would clutter up the stage and might prove unwieldy in the allegretto passages. A compromise is therefore effected by personifying only the more graceful ones, like *S* and the lower-case *f*, and this means that a certain discrimination must be used in selecting the actors. It also means that a great many little girls are going to be disappointed and their mothers' feelings outraged.

Little Alice Withstanley is chosen to play the part of the *Craft Guild Movement in Industry*, showing the rise of coöperation and unity among the working-classes. She is chosen because she has blonde hair which can be arranged in braids down her back, obviously essential to a proper representation of industrial team-work as a moving force in the world's progress. It so happens, however, that the daughter of the man who is cast for *Humidity* has had her eyes on this ingénue part ever since the printed text was circulated and had virtually been promised it by the Head of the House Committee of the Country Club, through whose kindness the grounds were to be used for the performance. There is a heated discussion over the merits of the two contestants between Mrs. Withstanley and the mother of the betrayed girl, which results in the withdrawal of the latter's offer to furnish Turkish rugs for the Oriental Decadence scene.

Following this, the rougher element of the community—enlisted to take part in the scenes showing

"There is a heated discussion between Mrs. Withstanley and the mother of the betrayed girl."

the building of the Pyramids and the first Battle of Bull Run—appear at one of the early rehearsals in a state of bolshevik upheaval, protesting against the unjust ruling which makes them attend all rehearsals and wait around on the side hill until their scenes are on, keeping them inactive sometimes from two to three hours, according to the finish with which the principals get through the prologue and opening scenes showing the Creation. The proletariat present an ultimatum, saying that the Committee in charge can either shorten their waiting hours or remove the restrictions on crap-shooting on the side-hill during their periods of inaction.

There is a meeting of the Director and his assistants who elect a delegation to confer with the striking legionaries, with the result that no compromise is reached, the soviet withdraws from the masque in a body, threatening to set fire to the grass on the first night of the performance.

During the rehearsals the husband of the woman who is portraying *Winter Wheat* is found wandering along the brookside with her sister cereal *Spring Wheat*, which, of course, makes further polite cooperation between these two staples impossible, and the Dance of the Food Stuffs has to be abandoned at the last moment. This adds to the general tension.

Three nights before the first performance the Director calls every one to a meeting in the trophy room of the Club-house and says that, so far as he is concerned, the show is off. He has given up his time to come out here, night after night, in an attempt to put on a masque that will be a credit to the community and a significant event in the world of art, and what has he found? Indifference, irresponsibility, lack of coöperation, non-attendance at rehearsals, and a spirit of *laissez-faire* in the face of which it is impossible to produce a successful masque. Consideration for his own reputation, as well as that of the township, makes it necessary

" The audience is composed chiefly of the aged and the infirm."

for him to throw the whole thing over, here and now.

The Chairman of the Committee then gets up and cries a little, and says that he is sure that if every one agrees to pull together during these last three days and to attend rehearsals faithfully and to try to get plenty of sleep, Mr. Parsleigh, the coach, will consent to help them through with the performance, and he asks every one who is willing to coöperate to say " Aye." Every one says " Aye " and Mr. Parsleigh is won over.

As for the masque itself, it is given, of course; and as most of the able-bodied people of the community are taking part, the audience is composed chiefly of the aged and the infirm, who catch muscular rheumatism from sitting out-of-doors and are greatly bored, except during those scenes when their relatives are taking part. The masque is hailed as a great success, however, in spite of the fact that the community has been disrupted and social life made impossible until the next generation grows up and agrees to let bygones be bygones.

But as a substitute for war, it has no equal.

XIII

CALL FOR MR. KENWORTHY!

A GREAT many people have wondered to themselves, in print, just where the little black laundry-studs go after they have been yanked from the shirt. Others pass this by as inconsequential, but are concerned over the ultimate disposition of all the pencil stubs that are thrown away. Such futile rumination is all well enough for those who like it. As for me, give me a big, throbbing question like this: " Who are the people that one hears being paged in hotels? Are they real people or are they decoys? And if they are real people, what are they being paged for? "

Now, there's something vital to figure out. And the best of it is that it *can* be figured out by the simple process of following the page to see whether he ever finds any one.

In order that no expense should be spared, I picked out a hotel with poor service, which means that it was an expensive hotel. It was so expensive that all you could hear was the page's voice as he walked by you; his footfalls made no noise in the extra heavy Bokhara. It was just a mingling of floating voices, calling for " Mr. Bla-bla, Mr. Schwer-a-a, Mr. Twa-a-a."

Out of this wealth of experimental material I picked a boy with a discouraged voice like Wallace Eddinger's, who seemed to be saying " I'm calling these names—because that's my job—if I wasn't calling these—I'd be calling out cash totals in an honor system lunchery—but if any one should ever answer to one of these names—I'd have a poor spell."

Allowing about fifteen feet distance between us for appearance's sake, I followed him through the lobby. He had a bunch of slips in his hand and from these he read the names of the pagees.

" Call for Mr. Kenworthy—Mr. Shriner—Mr. Bodkin—Mr. Blevitch—Mr. Kenworthy—Mr. Bodkin—Mr. Kenworthy—Mr. Shriner—call for Mr. Kenworthy—Mr. Blevitch—Mr. Kenworthy."

Mr. Kenworthy seemed to be standing about a 20 per cent better chance of being located than any of the other contestants. Probably the boy was of a romantic temperament and liked the name. Sometimes that was the only name he would call for mile upon mile. It occurred to me that perhaps Mr. Kenworthy was the only one wanted, and that the

[131]

"Sometimes that was the only name he would call for mile upon mile."

other names were just put in to make it harder, or
to give body to the thing.

But when we entered the bar the youth shifted
his attack. The name of Kenworthy evidently had
begun to cloy. He was fed up on romance and
wanted something substantial, homely, perhaps, but
substantial.

So he dropped Kenworthy and called: " Mr.
Blevitch. Call for Mr. Blevitch—Mr. Shriner—Mr.
Bodkin—Mr. Blevitch—"

But even this subtle change of tactics failed to net
him a customer. We had gone through the main
lobby, along the narrow passage lined with young
men waiting on sofas for young women who would
be forty minutes late, through the grill, and now
had crossed the bar, and no one had raised even an
eyebrow. No wonder the boy's voice sounded discouraged.

As we went through one of the lesser dining-
rooms, the dining-room that seats a lot of heavy men
in business suits holding cigarettes, who lean over
their plates the more confidentially to converse with
their blond partners, in this dining-room the plain-
tive call drew fire. One of the men in business
suits, who was at a table with another man and two
women, lifted his head when he heard the sound
of names being called.

"Boy!" he said, and waved like a traffic officer signaling, "Come!"

Eagerly the page darted forward. Perhaps this was Mr. Kenworthy! Or better yet, Mr. Blevitch.

"Anything here for Studz?"

"Anything here for Studz?" said the man in the business suit, when he was sure that enough people were listening.

"No, sir," sighed the boy. "Mr. Blevitch, Mr. Kenworthy, Mr. Shriner, Mr. Bodkin?" he suggested, hopefully.

"Naw," replied the man, and turned to his associates with an air of saying: " Rotten service here —just think of it, no call for me! "

On we went again. The boy was plainly skeptical. He read his lines without feeling. The management had led him into this; all he could do was to take it with as good grace as possible.

He slid past the coat-room girl at the exit (no small accomplishment in itself) and down a corridor, disappearing through a swinging door at the end. I was in no mood to lose out on the finish after following so far, and I dashed after him.

The door led into a little alcove and another palpitating door at the opposite end showed me where he had gone. Setting my jaw for no particular reason, I pushed my way through.

At first, like the poor olive merchant in the Arabian Nights I was blinded by the glare of lights and the glitter of glass and silver. Oh, yes, and by the snowy whiteness of the napery, too. " By the napery of the neck " wouldn't be a bad line to get off a little later in the story. I'll try it.

At any rate, it was but the work of a minute for me to realize that I had entered by a service entrance into the grand dining-room of the establishment, where, if you are not in evening dress, you are left to munch bread and butter until you starve to death and are carried out with your heels dragging, like the uncouth lout that you are. It was, if I may be allowed the phrase, a galaxy of beauty, with every one dressed up like the pictures. And I had entered 'way up front, by the orchestra.

Now, mind you, I am not ashamed of my gray suit. I like it, and my wife says that I haven't had anything so becoming for a long time. But in it I didn't check up very strong against the rest of the boys in the dining-room. As a gray suit it is above reproach. As a garment in which to appear single-handed through a trapdoor before a dining-room of well dressed Middle Westerners it was a fizzle from start to finish. Add to this the items that I had to snatch a brown soft hat from my head when I found out where I was, which caused me to drop the three evening papers I had tucked under my arm, and you will see why my up-stage entrance was the signal for the impressive raising of several dozen eyebrows, and why the captain approached me just exactly as one man approaches another when he is going to throw him out.

(Blank space for insertion of "napery of neck" line, if desired. Choice optional with reader.)

I saw that anything that I might say would be used against me, and left him to read the papers I had dropped. One only lowers one's self by having words with a servitor.

CALL FOR MR. KENWORTHY!

Gradually I worked my way back through the swinging doors to the main corridor and rushed down to the regular entrance of the grand dining-salon, to wait there until my quarry should emerge. Suppose he should find all of his consignees in this dining-room! I could not be in at the death then, and would have to falsify my story to make any kind of ending at all. And that would never do.

Once in a while I would catch the scent, when, from the humming depths of the dining-room, I could hear a faint " Call for Mr. Kenworthy " rising above the click of the oyster shells and the soft crackling of the "potatoes Julienne" one against another. So I knew that he had not failed me, and that if I had faith and waited long enough he would come back.

And, sure enough, come back he did, and without a name lost from his list. I felt like cheering when I saw his head bobbing through the mêlée of waiters and 'bus-boys who were busy putting clean plates on the tables and then taking them off again in eight seconds to make room for more clean plates. Of all discouraging existences I can imagine none worse than that of an eternally clean plate. There can be no sense of accomplishment, no glow of duty done, in simply being placed before a man and then taken away again. It must be almost as

[137]

bad as paging a man who you are sure is not in the hotel.

The futility of the thing had already got on the page's nerves, and in a savage attempt to wring a little pleasure out of the task he took to welding the names, grafting a syllable of one to a syllable of another, such as " Call for Mr. Kenbodkin—Mr. Shrineworthy—Mr. Blevitcher."

This gave us both amusement for a little while, but your combinations are limited in a thing like that, and by the time the grill was reached he was saying the names correctly and with a little more assurance.

It was in the grill that the happy event took place. Mr. Shriner, the one of whom we expected least, suddenly turned up at a table alone. He was a quiet man and not at all worked up over his unexpected honor. He signaled the boy with one hand and went on taking soup with the other, and learned, without emotion, that he was wanted on the telephone. He even made no move to leave his meal to answer the call, and when last seen he was adding pepper with one hand and taking soup with the other. I suspect that he was a " plant," or a plain-clothes house detective, placed there on purpose to deceive me.

We had been to every nook of the hotel by this

time, except the writing-room, and, of course, no one would ever look there for patrons of the hotel. Seeing that the boy was about to totter, I went up and spoke to him. He continued to totter, thinking, perhaps, that I was Mr. Kenworthy, his long-lost beau-ideal. But I spoke kindly to him and offered him a piece of chocolate almond-bar, and soon, in true reporter fashion, had wormed his secret from him before he knew what I was really after.

The thing I wanted to find out was, of course, just what the average is of replies to one paging trip. So I got around it in this manner: offering him another piece of chocolate almond-bar, I said, slyly: " Just what is the average number of replies to one paging trip? "

I think that he had suspected something at first, but this question completely disarmed him, and, leaning against an elderly lady patron, he told me everything.

" Well," he said, " it's this way: sometimes I find a man, and sometimes I can go the rounds without a bite. To-night, for instance, here I've got four names and one came across. That's about the average—perhaps one in six."

I asked him why he had given Mr. Kenworthy such a handicap at the start.

OF ALL THINGS!

A faint smile flickered across his face and then flickered back again.

"I call the names I think will be apt to hang round in the part of the hotel I'm in. Mr. Kenworthy would have to be in the dressy dining-room or in the lobby where they wait for ladies. You'd never find him in the bar or the Turkish baths. On the other hand, you'll never find a man by the name of Blevitch anywhere except in the bar. Of course, I take a chance and call every name once in so often, no matter where I am, but, on the whole, I uses my own discretion."

I gave him another piece of chocolate and the address of a good bootmaker and left him. What I had heard had sobered me, and the lights and music suddenly seemed garish. It is no weak emotion to feel that you have been face to face with a mere boy whose chances of success in his work are one to six.

And I found that he had not painted the lily in too glowing terms. I followed other pages that night—some calling for "Mr. Strudel," some for "Mr. Carmickle," and one was broad-minded enough to page a "Mrs. Bemis." But they all came back with that wan look in their eyes and a break in their voices.

And each one of them was stopped by the man in the business suit in the downstairs dining-room and each time he considered it a personal affront that there wasn't a call for " Studz."

Some time I'm going to have him paged, and when he comes out I shall untie his necktie for him.

XIV

FOOTBALL; COURTESY OF MR. MORSE

SUNDAY morning these fine fall days are taken up with reading about the " 40,000 football enthusiasts " or the " gaily-bedecked crowd of 60,000 that watched the game on Saturday." And so they probably did, unless there were enough men in big fur coats who jumped up at every play and yelled " Now we're off! " thus obstructing the view of an appreciable percentage.

But why stop at the mention of the paltry 50,000 who sat in the Bowl or the Stadium? Why forget the twice 50,000 all over the country, in Chicago, St. Louis, San Francisco, Atlanta, who watched the same game over the ticker, or sat in a smoke-fogged room listening to telegraphic announcements, play by play, or who even stood on the curbing in front of a newspaper office and watched an impartial cmployee shove a little yellow ball along a blackboard, usually indicating the direction in which the real football was *not* going. Since it is so important to give the exact number of people who saw the

game, why not do the thing up right and say: " Re-
turns which are now coming in from the Middle
West, with some of the rural districts still to be
heard from, indicate that at least 145,566 people
watched the Yale-Princeton football game yesterday. Secretary Dinwoodie of the San Francisco
Yale Club telegraphed late last night that the final
count in that city would probably swell the total to
a round 150,395. This is, or will be, the largest
crowd that ever assembled in one country to watch
a football game."

And watching the game in this vicarious manner
isn't so bad as the fellow who has got tickets and
carfare to the real game would like to have it. You
are in a warm room, where you can stretch your
legs and regulate your remarks to the intensity of
your emotions rather than to the sex of your neighbors. And as for thrills! " Dramatic suspense "
was probably first used as a term in connection with
this indoor sport.

The scene is usually some college club in the city
—a big room full of smoke and graduates. At one
end is a score-board and miniature gridiron, along
which a colored counter is moved as the telegraph
behind the board clicks off the plays hot from the
real gridiron. There is also an announcer, who, by
way of clarifying the message depicted on the

board, reads the wrong telegram in a loud, clear tone.

Just as the crowd in the football arena are crouching down in their fur coats the better to avoid watching the home team fumble the kick-off, the crowds two and ten hundred miles away are settling back in their chairs and lighting up the old pipes, while the German-silver-tongued announcer steps to the front of the platform and delivers the following:

" Yale won the toss and chose to defend the south goal, Princeton taking the west."

This mistake elicits much laughter, and a witty graduate who has just had lunch wants to know, as one man to the rest of the house, if it is puss-in-the-corner that is being played.

The instrument behind the board goes " Tick-ity-tick-tick-tickity."

There is a hush, broken only by the witty graduate, who, encouraged by his first success, wants to know again if it is puss-in-the-corner that is being played. This fails to gain.

" Gilblick catches the kick-off and runs the ball back to his own 3-yard line, where he is downed in his tracks," comes the announcement.

There is a murmur of incredulity at this. The little ball on the board shoots to the middle of the field.

" Hey, how about that? " shout several precincts.

The announcer steps forward again.

" That was the wrong announcement," he admits. " Tweedy caught the kick-off and ran the ball back twenty-five yards to midfield, where he is thrown for a loss. On the next play there was a forward pass, Klung to Breakwater, which—"

Here the message stops. Intense excitement.

" Tickity-tickity-tick-tickity."

The man who has $5 on the game shuts his eyes and says to his neighbor: " I'll bet it was intercepted."

A wait of two triple-space minutes while the announcer winds his watch. Then he steps forward. There is a noisy hush.

" It is estimated that 50,000 people filed into the Palmer Stadium to-day to watch Yale and Princeton in their annual gridiron contest," he reads. " Yale took the field at five minutes of 2, and was greeted by salvos and applause and cheering from the Yale section. A minute later the Princeton team appeared, and this was a signal for the Princeton cohorts to rise as one man and give vent to their famous ' Undertaker's Song.' "

" How about that forward pass? " This, as one man, from the audience.

The ball quivers and starts to go down the field.

OF ALL THINGS!

A mighty shout goes up. Then something happens, and the ball stops, looks, listens and turns in the other direction. Loud groans. A wooden slide in the mechanism of the scoreboard rattles into place, upside down. Agile spectators figure out that it says " Pass failed."

Every one then sinks back and says, " They ought not to have tried that." If the quarterback could hear the graduates' do-or-die backing of their team at this juncture he would trot into the locker building then and there.

Again the clear voice from the platform:

" Tweedy punts—" (noisy bond-salesman in back of room stands up on a chair and yells " Yea! " and is told to " Shut up " by three or four dozen neighbors) " to Gumble on his 15-yard line. Gumble fumbles."

The noisy bond-salesman tries to lead a cheer but is prevented.

Frightful tension follows. Who recovered? Whose ball is it? On what line? Wet palms are pressed against trouser legs. How about it?

" Tick-tickity-tick-tickity-tickity-tickity."

You can hear the announcer's boots squeak as he steps forward.

" Mr. A. T. Blevitch is wanted on the telephone," he enunciates.

FOOTBALL

Mr. A. T. Blevitch becomes the most unpopular man in that section of the country. Every one turns to see what a man of his stamp can look like. He is so embarrassed that he slinks down in his seat and refuses to answer the call.

"Noisy bond-salesman in back of room
stands up on chair and yells 'Yea!'"

"Klung goes around right end for a gain of two yards," is the next message from the front.

The bond-salesman shouts "Yea!"

OF ALL THINGS!

" How about that fumble? " shouts every one else.

The announcer goes behind the scenes to talk it over with the man who works the Punch-and-Judy, and emerges, smiling.

" In the play preceding the one just announced," he says, " Gumble fumbled and the ball was re-covered by Breakwater, who ran ten yards for a touchdown—"

Pandemonium! The bond-salesman leads himself in a cheer. The witty man says, " Nothing to it."

There is comparative quiet again, and every one lights up the old pipes that have gone out.

The announcer steps forward with his hand raised as if to regulate traffic.

" There was a mistake in the announcement just made," he says pleasantly. " In place of ' touch-down ' read ' touchback.' The ball is now in play on the 20-yard line, and Kleenwell has just gone through center for three yards."

By this time no one in the audience has any defi-nite idea of where the ball is or who has it. On the board it is hovering between midfield and second base.

" On the next play Legly punts—"

" Block that punt! Block that punt! " warns the bond-salesman, as if it were the announcer who was opposing Legly.

FOOTBALL

" Sit down, you poor fish! " is the consensus of opinion.

" Legly punts to Klung on the latter's 25-yard line, where the first period ends."

And so it goes throughout the game; the announcer calling out gains and the dummy football registering corresponding losses; Messrs. A. T. Blevitch and L. H. Yank being wanted on the telephone in the middle of forward passes; the noisy person in the back of the room yelling " Yea " on the slightest provocation and being hushed up at each outbreak; and every one wondering what the quarterback meant by calling for the plays he did.

In smaller cities, where only a few are gathered together to hear the results, things are not done on such an elaborate scale. The dummy gridiron and the dummy announcer are done away with and the ten or a dozen rooters cluster about the news ticker, most of them with the intention of watching for just a few minutes and then going home or back to the office. And they always wait for just one more play, shifting from one foot to the other, until the game is over.

About a ticker only the three or four lucky ones can see the tape. The rest have to stand on tip-toe and peer over the shoulders of the man in front. They don't care. Some one will always read the results aloud, just as a woman will read aloud the

cut-ins at the movies. The one who is doing the
reading usually throws in little advance predictions
of his own when the news is slow in coming, with
the result that those in the back get the impression
that the team has at least a " varied attack," effect-
ing at times a field goal and a forward pass in the
same play.

A critical period in the game, as it comes dribbling
in over the ticker, looks something like this:

YALE . PRINCTON . GAME. . . . CHEKFMKL
. . . . KLUNG . GOES . AROUND . LEFT .
END . FOR . A . GAIN . OF . YDS. . . . . . . A
. FORWARD . PASS . TWEEDY . TO . KLUNG
. NETS. . . . . (Ticker stops ticking).

Murmurs of " Come on, there, whasser matter? "

Some one suggests that the pass was illegal and
that the whole team has been arrested.

The ticker clears its throat. Br-r-r-r-r-r-r-r-r-r

The ticker stabs off a line of dots and begins:

" BOWIE . FIRST . RACE. . MEASLES . FIRST
. . 13.60 . . AND . . 6.00 . . WHORTLEBERRY .
SCND . PLACE . 3.80 . . EMMA GOLDMAN,
THIRD. . TIME . 1.09.4.5. . NON . START .
PROCRASTINATION . UNCLE TOM'S CABIN "

A few choice remarks are passed in the privacy
of the little circle, to just the effect that you would
suspect.

A newcomer elbows his way in and says: " What's

the good word? Any score yet?" and some one replies: "Yes. The score now stands 206 to o in favor of Notre Dame." This grim pleasantry is expressive of the sentiment of the group toward new-comers. It is each man for himself now.

Br-r-r-r-r-r-r-r-r-r-r-r-r-r-r-r-r!

"Here she comes, now!" whispers the man who is hanging over the glass news terminal, reading aloud: "Yale-Princeton-Game-Second Quarter (Good-night, what became of that forward pass in the first quarter?) Yale's - ball - in - mid - field - Hornung - takes - ball - around - left - end - making - it - first - down - Tinfoil - drops - back - for - a - try - at - a - field - goal. (Oh, boy! Come on, now!)"

"Why the deuce do they try a field goal on the first down?" asks a querulous graduate-strategist. "Now, what he ought to do is to keep a-plugging there at tackle, where he has been going—"

Br-r-r-r-r-r-r-r-r-r-r-r-r-r-r-r-r!

"Bet he missed it!" offers some one with vague gambling instincts.

"..INS. NEEDLES..1¼..ZINC..CON..4½ ..WASHN..THE CENSUS . OFFICE . ESTI-MATES . THE CONSUMPTION . OF COTTON . WASTE . IN . THE . MFGR . OF . AUTO-MBLE . HOODS . AS . 66.991.059 LBS. . IN-CLUDING . LINTERS . AND . HULL ◙ FIBER.."

OF ALL THINGS!

And just then some one comes in from the outside, all fresh and disagreeably cheery, and wants to know what the score is and if there have been many forward passes tried and who is playing quarter for Yale, and if any one has got a cigarette.

It is really just the same sort of program as obtains in the big college club, only on a small scale. They are all watching the same game and they are all wishing the same thing and before their respective minds' eyes is the picture of the same stadium, with the swarm of queen bees and drones clinging to its sides. And every time that you, who are one of the cold and lucky ones with a real ticket, see a back break loose for a long run and hear the explosion of hoarse shouts that follows, you may count sixty and then listen to hear the echo from every big city in the country where the old boys have just got the news.

XV

A LITTLE DEBIT IN YOUR TONNEAU

MOTORISTS, as a class, are not averse to public discussion of their troubles. In fact, one often wonders how some of them ever get time to operate their cars, so tied up do they seem to be with these little experience-meetings, at which one man tells, with appropriate gestures, how he ran out of gas between Springfield and Worcester, while another gives a perfect bit of character acting to show just how the policeman on the outskirts of Trenton behaved.

But there seems to be one phase of the motorist's trials which he never bares to the public. He will confide to you just how bad the gasoline was that he bought at the country garage; he will make it an open secret that he had four blow-outs on the way home from the country-club; but of one of his most poignant sorrows he never speaks. I refer to the guests who snuggle in his tonneau.

Probably more irritations have arisen from the tonneau than from the tires, day in and day out, and yet you never hear a man say, " Well, I certainly had an unholy crew of camp-followers out with me to-day—friends of my wife." Say what you will, there is an innate delicacy in the average motorist, or such repression could not be.

Consider the types of tonneau guests. They are as generic and fundamental as the spectrum and you will find them in Maine and New Mexico at the same time.

There is the first, or major, classification, which may be designated as the Financially Paralyzed. Persons in this class, on stepping into your machine, automatically transfer all their money troubles to you. You become, for the duration of the ride, whether it be to the next corner or to Palm Beach, their financial guardian, and any little purchases which are incidental to the trip (such as three meals a day) belong to your list of running expenses." There seems to be something about the motion of the automobile that inhibits their ability to reach for their purses, and they become, if you want to be poetical about it, like clay in the hands of the potter. Whither thou goest they will go; thy check-book is their check-book. It is just like the one great, big, jolly family—of which you are the father and backer.

Such people always make a great to-do about starting off on a trip. You call for them and they appear at the window and wave, to signify that they see you, and go through motions to show that just as soon as Clara has put on her leggings they will be down. Soon they appear, swathed in a tremendous quantity of motor wraps and veils (you can usually tell the guests in a car by the number of head-veils they wear) and get halfway down the walk, when Clara remembers her rain-coat and has to swish back upstairs, veils and all. Out again, and just as they get wedged into the tonneau, the elderly guest wonders if there is time for some one to run in again and tell Helma that if the Salvation Army man comes for the old magazines she is to tell him to come again to-morrow. By the time this message is relayed to Helma Garcia one solid half-hour has been dissipated from the cream of the morning. This does not prevent the guests from remarking, as the motor starts, that it certainly is a heavenly day and that it couldn't have been better if it had been ordered. Knowing the type, you can say to yourself that if the day *had* been ordered you know who would have had to give the order and pay the check.

From that time on, you are the moneyed interest behind the venture. Meals at road-houses, toll charges, evening papers, hot chocolates at the country drug store, hair net for Clara, and, of course, a liberal injection of gasoline on the way home, all of these items and about fourteen others come in your bailiwick. The guests have been asked out for a ride, and "findings is keepings." If you have money enough to run a car, you probably have money enough to support them for a day or so. That's only fair, isn't it?

"He always has a quip to snap at you to keep you cheered up."

Under a sub-head (a), in this same category, come the guests who are stricken with *rigor mortis* when there are any repairs to be made about the machine. Male offenders in this line are, of course, the only ones that can be dealt with here; putting on a tire is no job for women and children. But the man who is the life of the party in the tonneau throughout the trip, who thinks nothing of climbing all over the back of the car in imitation of a Roman charioteer, will suddenly become an advocate of the basic eight-hour working day which began just eight hours before, whenever there is a man's work to be done on one of the tires. He will watch you while you work, and always has a good word to say or a quip to snap at you to keep you cheered up, but when it comes to taking off his coat and lending a hand at the jack he is an Oriental incense-holder on the guest-room mantel. He admits in no uncertain tones, that he is a perfect dub when it comes to handling machinery and that he is more apt to be in the way at a time like this than not. And maybe he is right, after all.

We next come to the class of tonneau-freight who are great believers in what Professor Muensterberg called "Auto-Suggestion." These people, although not seated in the driver's seat, have their own ideas on driving and spare no pains to put their theories in the form of suggestions. In justice to the Great Army of the Unemployed known as "guests" it must be admitted that a large percentage of these suggestions emanate from some member of the owner's family and not from outsiders. It is very often Mrs. Wife who is off-side in this play, but as she is usually in the tonneau, she comes under the same classification.

There are various ways of framing suggestions to the driver from the back seat. They are all equally annoying. Among the best are:

"For heaven's sake, George, turn in a little. There is a car behind that wants to pass us."

"Look out where you're going, Stan."

"Henry, if you don't slow down I'm going to get out and take the train back home."

"If this is accompanied with a clutching gesture at the driver's arm, it is sure to throw him into a good humor."

If this is accompanied by a clutching gesture at the driver's arm it is sure to throw him into a good humor for the rest of the trip, so that a good time will be had by all present.

Although guests are not so prone to make suggestions on the running of the car as are those who, through the safety of family connection, may do so without fear of bodily assault from the driver, nevertheless, a guest may, according to the code, lean over the back of the seat and slip little hints as to the route. Especially if one of them be entrusted with a Blue Book does this form of auto-suggestion become chronic.

"It says here that we should have taken that road

to the right back there by the Soldiers' Monument," informs the reader over your shoulder. Or—

" Somehow this doesn't seem like the right road. Personally, I think that we ought to turn around and go back to the cross-roads."

If it is Mrs. Wife in the tonneau who has her own ideas on the route, you might as well give in at her first suggestion, for the risk that she is right is too great to run. If she says that she would advise taking the lane that runs around behind that school-house, take it. Then, if it turns out to be a blind alley, you have the satisfaction of saying nothing, very eloquently and effectively. But if you refuse to take her suggestion, and *your* road turns out to be even halfway wrong, you might as well turn the wheel over to your little son and go South for the winter, for you will never hear the ultimate cry of triumph. Your season will practically be ruined. I can quote verbatim from the last affair of this kind:

(Voice from the tonneau): " Albert, I think we ought to have taken the road at the left."

" No, we hadn't."

" I'm sure of it. I saw a sign which said: ' Paxton ' on it."

" No, you didn't."

" Well, you wait and see."

" I'm waiting."

There is a silence for ten minutes, while the car jounces along a road which gets narrower and rockier.

(Voice from the tonneau): " I suppose you think this is the way to Paxton? "

" I certainly *do*."

" Oh, you make me sick! "

Silence and jounces.

Sudden stop as the road ends at a silo.

" I beg your pardon [addressed to a rustic], which is the road to Paxton? "

" Paxton? "

" Yes."

" The road to Paxton? "

" Yes."

" Well, you go back over the rud you just come over, about three mile, till you come to a rud turnin' off to the right with a sign which says ' Paxton.' "

(Voice from the tonneau, beginning at this point and continuing all of the way back, all the rest of the day and night, and until snow falls): " *There!* what did I tell you? But, oh no, you know it all. Didn't I tell you "—etc., etc.

On the whole, it would seem that the artists who draw the automobile advertisements make a mistake in drawing the tonneau so roomy and so full of people. There should be no tonneau.

XVI

A ROMANCE IN ENCYCLOPEDIA LAND

Written After Three Hours' Browsing in a New Britannica Set

PICTURE to yourself an early spring afternoon along the banks of the river Aa, which, rising in the Teutoburger Wald, joins the Werre at Herford and is navigable as far as St. Omer.

Branching *bryophytu* spread their flat, dorsiventral bodies, closely applied to the sub-stratum on which they grew, and leafy carophyllaceæ twined their sepals in prodigal profusion, lending a touch of color to the scene. It was clear that nature was in preparation for her estivation.

But it was not this which attracted the eye of the young man who, walking along the phonolithic formation of the river-

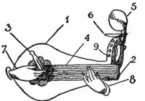

"Was playing softly to himself on a double curtail or converted bass-pommer."

bank, was playing softly to himself on a double curtail, or converted bass-pommer, an octave below the single curtail and therefore identical in pitch and construction with the early *fagotto* in C.

His mind was on other things.

He was evidently of Melanochronic extraction, with the pentagonal facial angle and strong obital ridges, but he combined with this the fine lines of a full-blooded native of Coll, where, indeed, he was born, seven miles west of Caliach Point, in Mull, and in full view of the rugged gneiss.

As he swung along, there throbbed again and again through his brain the beautiful opening paragraph of Frantisek Palacky's (1798-1876) *" Zur böhmischen Geschichtschreibung "* (Prague, 1871), written just after the author had refused a portfolio in the Pillersdorf Cabinet and had also declined to take part in the preliminary diet at Kromerice.

" If *he* could believe such things, why can not I? " murmured the young man, and crushed a ginkgo beneath his feet. Young men are often so. It is due to the elaterium of spring.

" By Ereshkigal," he swore softly to himself, " I'll do it."

No sooner had he spoken than he came suddenly out of the tangle of gymnosperms through whose leaves, needle-like and destitute of oil-glands as they were, he had been making his way, and emerged to a full view of the broad sweep of the Lake of Zug, just where the Lorze enters at its northern extremity and one and a quarter miles east of where it issues again to pursue its course toward the Reuss. Zug, at this point, is 1,368 feet above sea-level, and boasted its first steamer in 1852.

"Well," he sighed, as he gazed upon the broad area of subsidence, "if I were now an exarch, whose dignity was, at one time, intermediate between the Patriarchal and the Metropolitan and from whose name has come that of the politico-religious party, the Exarchists, I should not be here day-dreaming. I should be far away in Footscray, a city of Bourke County, Victoria, Australia, pop. (1901) 18,301."

"He came suddenly out of the tangle of gymnosperms."

And as he said this his eyes filled with tears, and under his skin, brown as fustic, there spread a faint flush, such as is often formed by citrocyde, or by pyrochloric acid when acting on uncured leather.

Far down in the valley the natives were celebrating the birthday of Gambrinus, a mythical Flemish king who is credited with the first brewing of beer. The sound of their voices set in motion longitudinal sound waves, and these, traveling through the surrounding medium, met the surface separating two media and were in part reflected, traveling back from the surface into the first medium again with the velocity with which they approached it, as depicted in Fig. 10. This caused the echo for which the Lake of Zug is justly famous.

The twilight began to deepen and from far above came the twinkling signals of, first, Böotes, then Coma Berenices, followed, awhile later, by Ursa Major and her little brother, Ursa Minor.

"The stars are clear to-night," he sighed. "I wonder if they are visible from the dacite elevation on which SHE lives."

His was an untrained mind. His only school had been the Eleatic School, the contention of which was that the true explanation of things lies in the conception of a universal unity of being, or the All-ness of One.

But he knew what he liked.

In the calm light of the stars he felt as if a uban had been lifted from his heart, 5 ubans being equal to 1 quat, 6 quats to 1 ammat and 120 ammats to 1 sos.

He was free again.

Turning, he walked swiftly down into the valley, passing returning peasants with their baa-poots, and

"She turned like a frightened aadvark." (Male, greatly reduced.)

soon came in sight of the shining lamps of the small but carefully built pooroos which lined the road.

Reaching the corner he saw the village epi peering over the tree-tops, and swarms of cicada, with the toothed famoras of their anterior legs mingling in a sleepy drone, like so many cichlids. It was all very home-like to the wanderer.

Suddenly there appeared on a neighboring eminence a party of guisards, such as, during the Saturnalia, and from the Nativity till the Epiphany were accustomed to disport themselves in odd costumes; all clad in clouting, and evidently returning from taking part in the celebration.

As they drew nearer,

"Barnaby Bernard Weenix." (1777-1829.)

[165]

our hero noticed a young woman in the front rank who was playing folk-songs on a cromorne with a double-reed mouth-piece enclosed in an air-reservoir.

"Why not to Wem?"
(From a contemporaneous print.)

In spite of the detritus wrought by the festival, there was something familiar about the buccinator of her face and her little mannerism of elevating her second phalanx. It struck him like the flash of a cloud highly charged by the coalescence of drops of vapor. He approached her, tenderly, reverently.

"Lange, Anne Françoise Elizabeth," he said, "I know you. You are a French actress, born in Genoa on the seventeenth of September, 1772, and you made your first appearance on the stage in *L'Ecossaise* in 1788. Your talent and your beauty gave you an enormous success in *Pamela*. It has taken me years to find you, but now we are united at last."

The girl turned like a frightened aard-vark, still

[166]

holding the cromorne in her hand. Then she smiled.

"Weenix, Barnaby Bernard (1777-1829)," she said very slowly, "you started business as a publisher in London about 1797."

They looked at each other for a moment in silence. He was the first to speak.

"Miss Lange, Anne," he said, "let us go together to Lar—and be happy there—happy as two ais, or three-toed South American sloths."

She lowered her eyes.

"I will go with you Mr. Weenix-Barney," she said, "to the ends of the earth. But why to Lar? Why not to Wem?"

"Because," said the young man, "Lar is the capital of Laristan, in 27 degrees, 30 minutes N., 180 miles from Shiraz, and contains an old bazaar consisting of four arcades each 180 feet long."

Their eyes met, and she placed her hands in his.

And, from the woods, came the mellow whinnying of a herd of vip, the wool of which is highly valued for weaving.

XVII

THE PASSING OF THE ORTHODOX PARADOX

WHATEVER irreparable harm may have been done to Society by the recent epidemic of crook, sex and other dialect plays, one great alleviation has resulted. They have driven up-stage, for the time being, the characters who exist on tea and repartee in "The drawing-room of Sir Arthur Peaversham's town house, Grosvenor Square. Time: late Autumn."

A person in a crook play may have talked underworld patois which no self-respecting criminal would have allowed himself to utter, but he did not sit on a divan and evolve abnormal *bons mots* with each and every breath. The misguided and misinformed daughter in the Self and Sex Play may have lisped words which only an interne should hear, but she did not offer a succession of brilliant but meaningless paradoxes as a substitute for real conversation.

Continuously snappy back-talk is now encountered chiefly in such acts as those of "Cooney & LeBlanc, the Eccentric Comedy Dancing Team."

And even *they* manage to scrape along without the paradoxes.

But there was a time, beginning with the Oscar Wilde era, when no unprotected thought was safe.

" Snappy back-talk is now encountered chiefly in such acts as ' Cooney and Le Blanc, the Eccentric Comedy Dancing Team.' "

It might be seized at any moment by an English Duke or a Lady Agatha and strangled to death. Even the butlers in the late 'eighties were wits, and served epigrams with cucumber sandwiches; and a person entering one of these drawing-rooms and talking in connected sentences—easily understood by everybody—each with one subject, predicate and meaning, would have been looked upon as a high class moron. One might as well have gone to a dinner at Lady Coventry's without one's collar, as without one's kit of trained paradoxes.

A late Autumn afternoon in one of these semi-

"The butlers served epigrams with the cucumber sandwiches."

Oscar Wilde plays, for instance, would run something like this:

SCENE—*The Octagon Room in Lord Raymond Eaveston's Manor House in Stropshire.*

LADY EAVESTON *and* SIR THOMAS WAFFLETON *are discovered, arranging red flowers in a vase.*

SIR T.: I detest red flowers; they are so yellow.

LADY E.: What a cynic you are, Sir Thomas. I really must not listen to you or I shall hear something that you say.

[170]

THE ORTHODOX PARADOX

SIR T.: Not at all, my dear Lady Eaveston. I detest people who listen closely; they are so inattentive.

LADY E.: Pray do not be analytical, my dear Sir Thomas. When people are extremely analytical with me I am sure that they are superficial, and, to me, nothing is more abominable than superficiality, unless perhaps it is an intolerable degree of thoroughness.

(*Enter Meadows, the Butler*)

MEADOWS (*announcing*): Sir Mortimer Longley and Mrs. Wrennington,—a most remarkable couple, —I may say in announcing them,—in that there is nothing at all remarkable about them.

(*Enter Sir Mortimer and Mrs. Wrennington*)

MRS. W.: So sorry to be late, dear Lady Eaveston. But it is so easy to be on time that I always make it a point to be late. It lends poise, and poise is a charming quality for any woman to have, am I not right, Sir Thomas?

SIR T.: You are always right, my dear Mrs. Wrennington, and never more so than now, for I know of no more attractive attribute than poise, unless perhaps it be embarrassment.

[171]

OF ALL THINGS!

LADY E.: What horrid cynics you men are! Really, Sir Thomas, one might think, from your sophisticated remarks that you had been brought up in the country and had seen nothing of life.

SIR T.: And so I *have* been, my dear Lady Eaveston. To my mind, London is nothing but the country, and certainly Stropshire is nothing but a metropolis. The difference is, that when one is in town, one lives with others, and when one is in the country, others live with one. And both plans are abominable.

MRS. W.: What a horrid combination! I hate horrid combinations; they always turn out to be so extremely pleasant.

(*Enter Meadows*)

MEADOWS (*announcing*): Sir Roland Pinshamton; Viscount Lemingham; Countess Trotski and Mr. Peters. In announcing these parties I cannot refrain from remarking that it has always been my opinion that a man who intends to get married should either know something or nothing, preferably both.

(*Exit Meadows*)

COUNTESS T.: So sorry to be late, my dear Lady Eaveston. It was charmingly tolerant of you to have us.

THE ORTHODOX PARADOX

LADY E.: Invitations are never tolerant, my dear Countess; acceptances always are. But do tell me, how is your husband, the Count,—or perhaps he is no longer your husband. One never knows these days whether a man is his wife's husband or whether she is simply his wife.

COUNTESS T. (*lighting a cigarette*): Really, Lady Eaveston, you grow more and more interesting. I detest interesting people; they are so hopelessly uninteresting. It is like beautiful people—who are usually so singularly unbeautiful. Has not that been your experience, Sir Mortimer?

SIR M.: May I have the pleasure of escorting you to the music-room, Mrs. Wrennington?

(*Exeunt omnes to music-room for dinner*)
Curtain.

It is from this that we have, in a measure, been delivered by the court-room scenes, and all the medical dramas. But the paradox still remains intrenched in English writing behind Mr. G. K. Chesterton, and he may be considered, by literary tacticians, as considerable stronghold.

Here again we find our commonplaces shaken up until they emerge in what looks like a new and tremendously imposing shape, and all of them ostensibly proving the opposite of what we have always

[173]

understood. If we do not quite catch the precise meaning at first reading, we lay it to our imperfect perception and try to do better on the next one. It seldom occurs to us that it really may have no meaning at all and never was intended to have any, any more than the act of hanging by your feet from parallel bars has any further significance than that you can manage to do it.

So, before retiring to the privacy of our personal couches, let us thank an all wise Providence, that the drama-paradox has passed away.

XVIII

SHAKESPEARE EXPLAINED

Carrying on the System of Footnotes to a Silly Extreme

PERICLES

Act II. Scene 3

Enter first Lady-in-Waiting (Flourish,[1] Hautboys[2] and[3] torches[4]).

First Lady-in-Waiting—What[5] ho![6]   Where[7] is[8] the[9] music?[10]

NOTES

1. *Flourish:* The stage direction here is obscure. Clarke claims it should read " flarish," thus changing the meaning of the passage to " flarish " (that is, the King's), but most authorities have agreed that it should remain " flourish," supplying the predicate which is to be flourished. There was at this time a custom in the countryside of England to flourish a mop as a signal to the passing vender of berries, signifying that in that particular household there was a consumer-demand for berries, and

this may have been meant in this instance. That
Shakespeare was cognizant of this custom of flour-
ishing the mop for berries is shown in a similar
passage in the second part of King Henry IV, where

"Might be one of the hautboys bearing a box
of "trognies" for the actors to suck.

he has the Third Page enter and say, "Flourish."
Cf. also Hamlet, IV, 7: 4.

2. *Hautboys*, from the French *haut*, meaning
"high" and the Eng. *boys*, meaning "boys." The
word here is doubtless used in the sense of "high
boys," indicating either that Shakespeare intended

to convey the idea of spiritual distress on the part of the First Lady-in-Waiting or that he did not. Of this Rolfe says: " Here we have one of the chief indications of Shakespeare's knowledge of human nature, his remarkable insight into the petty foibles of this work-a-day world." Cf. T. N. 4: 6, " Mine eye hath play'd the painter, and hath stell'd thy beauty's form in table of my heart."

3. *and*. A favorite conjunctive of Shakespeare's in referring to the need for a more adequate navy for England. Tauchnitz claims that it should be pronounced " und," stressing the anti-penult. This interpretation, however, has found disfavor among most commentators because of its limited significance. We find the same conjunctive in A. W. T. E. W. 6: 7, " Steel-boned, unyielding *and* uncomplying virtue," and here there can be no doubt that Shakespeare meant that if the King should consent to the marriage of his daughter the excuse of Stephano, offered in Act 2, would carry no weight.

4. *Torches*. The interpolation of some foolish player and never the work of Shakespeare (Warb.). The critics of the last century have disputed whether or not this has been misspelled in the original, and should read " trochies " or " troches." This might well be since the introduction of tobacco into England at this time had wrought havoc with the speak-

ing voices of the players, and we might well imagine
that at the entrance of the First Lady-in-Waiting
there might be perhaps one of the hautboys men-
tioned in the preceding passage bearing a box of
troches or " trognies " for the actors to suck. Of
this entrance Clarke remarks: " The noble mixture
of spirited firmness and womanly modesty, fine sense
and true humility, clear sagacity and absence of con-
ceit, passionate warmth and sensitive delicacy, generous love and self-diffidence with which Shakespeare
has endowed this First Lady-in-Waiting renders
her in our eyes one of the most admirable of his
female characters."   Cf. M. S. N. D. 8: 9, " That
solder'st close impossibilities and mak'st them kiss."

5. *What*—What.

6. *Ho!* In conjunction with the preceding word
doubtless means " What ho! " changed by Clarke to
" What hoo! " In the original ms. it reads " What
hi! " but this has been accredited to the tendency
of the time to write " What hi " when " what ho "
was meant. Techner alone maintains that it should
read " What humpf! " Cf. Ham. 5: 0, " High-ho! "

7. *Where.* The reading of the folio, retained by
Johnson, the Cambridge editors and others, but it
is not impossible that Shakespeare wrote " why,"
as Pope and others give it. This would make the
passage read " Why the music?" instead of " Where

is the music? " and would be a much more probable interpretation in view of the music of that time. Cf. George Ade. Fable No. 15, "Why the gunny-sack? "

8. *is*—is not. That is, would not be.

9. *the*. Cf. Ham. 4: 6. M. S. N. D. 3: 5. A. W. T. E. W. 2: 6. T. N. 1: 3 and Macbeth 3: 1, " that knits up *the* raveled sleeves of care."

10. *music*. Explained by Malone as " the art of making music " or " music that is made." If it has but one of these meanings we are inclined to think it is the first; and this seems to be favored by what precedes, " *the* music! " Cf. M. of V. 4: 2, " The man that hath no music in himself."

The meaning of the whole passage seems to be that the First Lady-in-Waiting has entered, concomitant with a flourish, hautboys and torches and says, " What ho!   Where is the music? "

XIX

THE SCIENTIFIC SCENARIO

SOONER or later some one is going to come out and say that the movies are too low-brow. I can just see it coming. Maybe some one has said it already, without its having been brought to my attention, as I have been very busy for the past two weeks on my yearly accounts (my accounts for the year 1920, I mean. What with one thing and another, I am a bit behind in my budget system).

And whenever this denouncement of the movies takes place, the first thing that is going to be specifically criticized is the type of story which is now utilized for scenarios. How can a nation hope to inject any culture in the minds of its people if it feeds them with moving-picture stories dealing with elemental emotions like love, hate, and a passion for evening-dress? Scenarios to-day have no cultural background. That's the trouble with them. They have no cultural background.

Now, if we are to make the movies count for anything in the mental development of our people, we must build them of sterner stuff. We must make them from stories and books which are of the mind rather than of the body. The action should be cerebral, rather than physical, and instead of thrilling at the sight of two horsemen galloping along a cliff, we should be given the opportunity of seeing two opposing minds doing a rough-and-tumble on the edge of a nice problem in Dialectics or Metaphysics.

I would suggest as a book, from which a pretty little scenario might be made, " The Education of Henry Adams." This volume has had a remarkable success during the past year among the highly educated classes. Public library records show that more people have lied about having read it than any other book in a decade. It contains five hundred pages of mental masochism, in which the author tortures himself for not getting anywhere in his brain processes. He just simply can't seem to get any further than the evolution of an elementary Dynamic Theory of History or a dilettante dabbling with a Law of Acceleration. And he came of a bright family, too.

I don't go in much for scenario writing myself, but I am willing to help along the cause of better moving-pictures by offering herewith an outline for a six-reel feature entitled " THE EDUCATION OF HENRY ADAMS; or WHY MINDS GO WRONG."

OF ALL THINGS!

CAST OF CHARACTERS

Henry Adams.
Left Frontal Brain Lobe.
Right Frontal Brain Lobe.
Manservant.
Crowd of Villagers, Reflexes, Complexes,
    and Mental Processes.

The first scene is, according to the decorated caption: " IN THE HARVARD COLLEGE STUDY OF HENRY ADAMS, SCION OF AN OLD NEW ENGLAND FAMILY, THE NIGHT BEFORE THE BIG CEREBRAL FUNCTION OF HIS YOUNG MANHOOD."

Henry Adams, a Junior, is discovered sitting at his desk in his room in Holworthy Hall. He has a notebook on the Glacial Period and Palæontology open in front of him. He is thinking of his Education. (*Flash-back showing courses taken since Freshman year. Pianist plays " Carry Me Back to Old Virginie.")* He bites his under lip and turns a page of his notes.

Caption: " DOES TRANSCENDENTALISM HOLD THE KEY? . . . I WONDER . . ."

(*Fade-out showing him biting his upper lip, still thinking.*)

The second scene is laid in Rome.

Caption: " HERE, AFTER A YEAR'S WANDERING

THE SCIENTIFIC SCENARIO

Through the Happy, Smiling Lands of Europe, Comes Young Henry Adams in His Search for Education. And Now, in the Shadow of An-

" Thrilling moment in 'The Education of Henry Adams.' "

cient Rome, He Finds Peace, but Not That Peace for Which He Sought."

He is discovered sitting on a rock among the ruins of the Capitol, thinking. He tosses a pebble from one hand to another and scowls. The shadows deepen, and he rises, passing his hand across his brow. (*Flash-back showing the Latin verbs which govern the dative case. Pianist plays: " The March of the Jolly Grenadiers."*)

He walks slowly to the *Museo Nazionale,* where

he stands pondering before a statue of Venus, thinking about Roman art and history—and about his Education.

Caption: "CAN ALL THIS BE FITTED INTO A TIME-SEQUENCE? CAN RIENZI, GARIBALDI, TIBERIUS GRACCHUS, AURELIAN, ANY OF THESE FAMOUS NAMES OF ROME, BE ADAPTED TO A SYSTEMATIC SCHEME OF EVOLUTION? NO, NO . . . A THOUSAND TIMES, NO! "

He sinks down on a rock and weeps bitterly.

The next scene is in England and our hero is found sitting at a desk in his study in London. He is gazing into space—thinking.

Caption: " AND SO, ALL THROUGH THE LONG, WEARY SUMMER, HENRY ADAMS SAT, HEAD IN HAND, WONDERING IF DARWIN WAS RIGHT. TO HIM THE GLACIAL EPOCH SEEMED LIKE A YAWNING CHASM BETWEEN A UNIFORMITARIAN WORLD AND HIMSELF. IF THE GLACIAL PERIOD WERE UNIFORMITY, WHAT WAS CATASTROPHE? . . . AND TO THIS QUESTION, THE COOL OF THE SUMMER'S EVENING IN SHROPSHIRE BROUGHT NO RELIEF."

He rises slowly and goes to the book-shelves, from which he draws a copy of " The Origin of Species." Placing it before him on the desk he turns the pages slowly until he comes to one which holds his attention.

THE SCIENTIFIC SCENARIO

Close-up of page 126, on which is read: " It is notorious that specific characters are more variable than generic. . . .

	Feet
Palæzoic strata (not including igneous beds)	57,154
Secondary strata	13,190
Tertiary strata	2,400 "

The book drops to the floor from his nerveless fingers and he buries his head in his arms, sobbing. (Music: " *When You and I Were Young, Maggie.*")

" TWENTY YEARS AFTER . . . HENRY ADAMS IS NO LONGER YOUNG, BUT IN HIS HEART LIES STILL THE HUNGER FOR EDUCATION. GOING FORWARD, EVER FORWARD, HE REALIZES AS NEVER BEFORE THAT WITHOUT THOUGHT IN THE UNIT, THERE CAN BE NO UNITY. THOUGHT ALONE IS FORM. MIND AND UNITY FLOURISH OR PERISH TOGETHER."

(*Allegorical flash-back showing Mind and Unity perishing together.*)

The hero is now seen seated in a Morris chair in Washington, touching his finger-tips together in a ruminative manner. Arising slowly, he goes to the window and looks out over Lafayette Square. Then he lights a cigar and goes back to his chair. He is pondering and attempting to determine when, between 3000 B.C. and 1000 A.D. the momentum of Europe was greatest, as exemplified in mathematics by such masters as Archimedes, Aristarchus, Ptolemy and Euclid.

(*Flash-back showing the mathematical theories of Archimedes, Aristarchus, Ptolemy and Euclid. Music: " Old Ireland Shall Be Free."*)

Rising from his chair again, he paces the floor, clenching his hands behind his back in mute fury.

Caption: " GOD HAVE MERCY ON ME! I CAN SEE IT ALL—I HAVE NEVER BEEN EDUCATED! "

NEXT WEEK: BERT LYTELL IN
" SARTOR RESARTUS "
A SMASHING SIX-REEL FEATURE
BY TOM CARLYLE

XX

THE MOST POPULAR BOOK OF THE MONTH

NEW YORK CITY (including all Boroughs) TELEPHONE DIRECTORY—N. Y. Telephone Co., N. Y. 1920. 8vo. 1208 pp.

IN picking up this new edition of a popular favorite, the reviewer finds himself confronted by a nice problem in literary ethics. The reader must guess what it is.

There may be said to be two classes of people in the world; those who constantly divide the people of the world into two classes, and those who do not. Both classes are extremely unpleasant to meet socially, leaving practically no one in the world whom one cares very much to know. This feeling is made poignant, to the point of becoming an obsession, by a careful reading of the present volume.

We are herein presented to some five hundred thousand characters, each one deftly drawn in a line or two of agate type, each one standing out from the rest in bold relief. It is hard to tell which one is the most lovable. In one mood we should say *W. S. Custard* of Minnieford Ave. In another, more susceptible frame of mind, we should stand by the character who opens the book and who first introduces us into this Kingdom of Make-Believe—

" The most popular book on earth."

Mr. V. Aagaard, the old " Impt. & Expt." How one seems to see him, impting and expting all the hot summer day through, year in and year out, always heading the list, but always modest and unassuming, always with a kindly word and a smile for passers-by on Broadway!

It is perhaps inaccurate to say that *V. Aagaard* introduces us to the book. He is the first flesh-and-blood human being with whom the reader comes in contact, but the initial place in the line should technically go to the A. & A. A. Excelsior Co. Having given credit where credit is due, however, let us express our personal opinion that this name is a mere trick, designed to crowd out all other competitors in the field for the honor of being in the premiere position, for it must be obvious to any one with any perception at all that the name doesn't make sense. *No* firm could be named the A. & A. A. Co., and the author of the telephone directory might better have saved his jokes until the body of the book. After all, Gelett Burgess does that sort of thing much better than any one else could hope to.

But, beginning with *V. Aagaard* and continuing through to *Mrs. L. Zyfers* of Yettman Ave., the reader is constantly aware of the fact that here are real people, living in a real city, and that they represent a problem which must be faced.

Sharp as we find the character etching in the book, the action, written and implied, is even more remarkable. Let us, for instance, take *Mr. Saml Dreylinger,* whose business is " Furn Reprg," or *Peter Shalijian,* who does " pmphlt bindg." Into whose experience do these descriptions not fit? The author need only mention a man bindg pmphlts to bring back a flood of memories to each and every one of us—perhaps our old home town in New England where bindg pmphlts was almost a rite during the long winter months, as well as a social function of no mean proportions. It is the ability to suggest, to insinuate, these automatic memories on the part of the reader without the use of extra words that makes the author of this work so worthy of the name of craftsman in the literary annals of the day.

Perhaps most deft of all is the little picture that is made of *Louise Winkler,* who is the village " sclp spclst." One does not have to know much medieval history to remember the position that the sclp spclst used to hold in the community during the Wars of the Roses. Or during Shay's Rebellion, for that matter. In those days, to be a sclp spclst was as important a post as that of " clb bdg stbls " (now done for New York City by Mr. Graham). People came from miles around to consult with the local sclp spclst on matters pertaining not only to sclps but to knt gds and wr whls, both of which departments of our daily life have now been delegated to separate agencies. Then gradually, with the growth of the trade guild movement, there came the Era of Specialization in Industry, and the high offices of the sclp spclst were dissipated among other trades, until only that coming strictly under the head of sclp speclzng remained. To this estate has *Miss*

Winkler come, and in that part of the book which deals with her and her work, we have, as it were, a little epic on the mutability of human endeavor. It is all too short, however, and we are soon thereafter plunged into the dreary round of expting and impting, this time through a character called *J. Wubbe,* who is interesting only in so far as he is associated with *M. Wrubel* and *A. N. Wubbenhorst,* all of whom come together at the bottom of the column.

The plot, in spite of whatever virtues may accrue to it from the acid delineation of the characters and the vivid action pictures, is the weakest part of the work. It lacks coherence. It lacks stability.

Perhaps this is because of the nature of the book itself. Perhaps it is because the author knew too well his Dunsany. Or his Wells. Or his Bradstreet. But it is the opinion of the present reviewer that the weakness of plot is due to the great number of characters which clutter up the pages. The Russian school is responsible for this. We see here the logical result of a sedulous aping of those writers such as Tolstoi, Andreief, Turgenief, Dostoiefsky, or even Pushkin, whose *metier* it was to fill the pages of their books with an inordinate number of characters, many of whom the reader was to encounter but once, let us say, on the Nevsky Prospekt or in the Smolny Institute, but all of whom added their peculiar names (we believe that we will not offend when we refer to Russian names as " peculiar ") to the general confusion of the whole.

In practice, the book is not flawless. There are five hundred thousand names, each with a corresponding telephone number. But, through some error in editing, the numbers are all wrong. Proof of this may be had by the simple expedient of calling up any one of the subscribers, using the number assigned by the author to that name. (Any name will do—let us say *Nicholas Wimpie*-Harlem 2131.) If the call is put in bright and early in the morning, the report will come over the wire just as the lights are going on for evening of the same day that " Harlem 2131 does not answer." The other numbers are invariably equally unproductive of results. The conclusion is obvious.

Aside from this point the book is a success.

XXI

CHRISTMAS AFTERNOON

Done in the Manner, if Not the Spirit, of Dickens

WHAT an afternoon! Mr. Gummidge said
that, in his estimation, there never had *been*
such an afternoon since the world began, a sentiment which was heartily endorsed by Mrs. Gummidge and all the little Gummidges, not to mention
the relatives who had come over from Jersey for
the day.

In the first place, there was the *ennui*. And such
ennui as it was! A heavy, overpowering *ennui*, such
as results from a participation in eight courses of
steaming, gravied food, topping off with salted nuts
which the little old spinster Gummidge from Oak
Hill said she never knew when to stop eating—
and true enough she didn't—a dragging, devitalizing
ennui, which left its victims strewn about the living-
room in various attitudes of prostration suggestive
of those of the petrified occupants in a newly un-
earthed Pompeiian dwelling; an *ennui* which carried with it a retinue of yawns, snarls and thinly

[193]

OF ALL THINGS!

"What an afternoon!"

veiled insults, and which ended in ruptures in the clan spirit serious enough to last throughout the glad new year.

Then there were the toys! Three and a quarter dozen toys to be divided among seven children. Surely enough, you or I might say, to satisfy the little tots. But that would be because we didn't know the tots. In came Baby Lester Gummidge, Lillian's boy, dragging an electric grain-elevator which happened to be the only toy in the entire collection which appealed to little Norman, five-year-old son of Luther, who lived in Rahway. In came curly-headed Effie in frantic and throaty disputation with Arthur, Jr., over the possession of an articulated zebra. In came Everett, bearing a mechanical negro which would no longer dance, owing to a previous forcible feeding by the baby of a marshmallow into its only available aperture. In came Fonlansbee, teeth buried in the hand of little Ormond, which bore a popular but battered remnant of what had once been the proud false-bosom of a hussar's uniform. In they all came, one after another, some crying, some snapping, some pulling, some pushing—all appealing to their respective parents for aid in their intra-mural warfare.

And the cigar smoke! Mrs. Gummidge said that she didn't mind the smoke from a good cigarette, but would they mind if she opened the windows for just a minute in order to clear the room of the heavy aroma of used cigars? Mr. Gummidge stoutly maintained that they were good cigars. His brother, George Gummidge, said that he, likewise, would say that they were. At which colloquial sally both the Gummidge brothers laughed testily, thereby breaking the laughter record for the afternoon.

Aunt Libbie, who lived with George, remarked from the dark corner of the room that it seemed just like Sunday to her. An amendment was offered to this statement by the cousin, who was in the insurance business, stating that it was worse than Sunday. Murmurings indicative of as hearty agreement with this sentiment as their lethargy would allow came from the other members of the family circle, causing Mr. Gummidge to suggest a walk in the air to settle their dinner.

And then arose such a chorus of protestations as has seldom been heard. It was too cloudy to walk. It was too raw. It looked like snow. It looked like rain. Luther Gummidge said that he must be starting along home soon, anyway, bringing forth the acid query from Mrs. Gummidge as to whether or not he was bored. Lillian said that she felt a cold coming on, and added that something they had had for dinner must have been undercooked. And so it went, back and forth, forth and back, up ana down, and in and out, until Mr. Gummidge's suggestion of a walk in the air was reduced to a tattered impossibility and the entire company glowed with ill-feeling.

In the meantime, we must not forget the children. No one else could. Aunt Libbie said that she didn't think there was anything like children to make a Christmas; to which Uncle Ray, the one with the Masonic fob, said, " No, thank God! " Although Christmas is supposed to be the season of good cheer, you (or I, for that matter) couldn't have told, from listening to the little ones, but what it was the children's Armageddon season, when Nature had decreed that only the fittest should survive, in order that the race might be carried on by the strongest, the most predatory and those possessing the best protective coloring. Although there were constant admonitions to Fonlansbee to " Let Ormond have that whistle now; it's his," and to Arthur, Jr., not to be selfish, but to " give the kiddie-car to Effie; she's smaller than you are," the net result was always that Fonlansbee kept the whistle and Arthur, Jr., rode in permanent, albeit disputed, possession of the kiddie-car. Oh, that we mortals should set ourselves up against the inscrutable workings of Nature!

OF ALL THINGS!

Hallo! A great deal of commotion! That was Uncle George stumbling over the electric train, which had early in the afternoon ceased to function and which had been left directly across the

"Hallo! A great deal of commotion!"

threshold. A great deal of crying! That was Arthur, Jr., bewailing the destruction of his already useless train, about which he had forgotten until the present moment. A great deal of recrimination! That was Arthur, Sr., and George fixing it up. And finally a great crashing! That was Baby Lester pulling over the tree on top of himself, necessitating the bringing to bear of all of Uncle Ray's knowledge of forestry to extricate him from the wreckage.

And finally Mrs. Gummidge passed the Christmas candy around. Mr. Gummidge afterward admitted that this was a tactical error on the part of his spouse. I no more believe that Mrs. Gummidge thought they wanted that Chrismas candy than I believe that she thought they wanted the cold turkey which she later suggested. My opinion is that she wanted to drive them home. At any rate, that is what she succeeded in doing. Such cries as there were of " Ugh! Don't let me see another thing to eat! " and " Take it away! " Then came hurried scramblings in the coat-closet for overshoes. There were the rasping sounds made by cross parents when putting wraps on children. There were insincere exhortations to " come and see us soon " and to " get together for lunch some time." And, finally, there were slammings of doors and the silence of utter exhaustion, while Mrs. Gummidge went about picking up stray sheets of wrapping paper.

And, as Tiny Tim might say in speaking of Christmas afternoon as an institution, " God help us, every one."

XXII

HAIL, VERNAL EQUINOX!

IF all that I hear is true, a great deal has been written, first and last, about that season which we slangily call " Spring "; but I don't remember ever having seen it done in really first-class form;— that is, in such a way that it left something with you to think over, something that you could put your finger on and say, " There, *there* is a Big, Vital Thought that I can carry away with me to my room."

What Spring really needs is a regular press-agent sort of write-up, something with the Punch in it, an article that will make people sit up and say to themselves, " By George, there must be something in this Spring stuff, after all."

What sort of popularity did Education have until correspondence schools and encyclopedias began to give publicity to it in their advertisements? Where would Music be to-day if it were not for the exhortations of the talking-machine and mechanical-piano companies telling, through their advertising-copy writers, of the spiritual exaltation that comes from a love of music? These things were all right in their way before the press-agent took hold of them, but they never could have hoped to reach their present position without him.

Of course, all this has just been leading up to the point I want to make,—that something more ought to be written about Spring. When you consider that every one, including myself, agrees that *nothing* more should be written about it, I think that I have done rather well to prove as much as I have so far. And, having got this deep into the thing, I can't very well draw back now.

Well then, Spring is a great season. Nobody will gainsay me that. Without it, we should crash right from Winter into Summer with no chance to shift to light-weight underwear. I could write a whole piece about that phase of it alone, and, if I were pressed for things to say, I myself could enlarge on it now, making up imaginary conversation of people who have been caught in balbriggans by the first sweltering day of summer. But I have so many more things to say about Spring that I can't stop to bother with deadwood like that. Such literary fillerbusting should be left to those who are not so full of their subject as I am.

In preparing for this article, I thought it best to look up a little on the technical side of Spring, about which so little is known, at least by me. And, would you believe it, the Encyclopedia Britannica, which claims in its advertisements not only to make its readers presidents of the Boards of Directors of any companies they may select, but also shows how easy it would be for Grandpa or Little Edna to carry the whole set about from room to room, if, by any possible chance they should ever want to, this same Encyclopedia Britannica makes no reference to Spring, except incidentally, along with Bed Springs and Bubbling Springs.

This slight of one of our most popular seasons is probably due to the fact that Spring is not exclusively a British product and was not invented by a Briton. Had Spring been fortunate enough to have had the Second Earl of Stropshire-Stropshire-Stropshire as one of its founders, the Britannica could probably have seen its way clear to give it a five-page article, signed by the Curator of the Jade Department in the British Museum, and illustrated with colored plates, showing the effect of Spring on the vertical and transverse sections of the stamen of the South African Euphorbiceæ.

I was what you might, but probably wouldn't, call stunned at not finding anything about the Season of Love in the encyclopedia, for without that assistance what sort of a scientific article could

HAIL, VERNAL EQUINOX!

I do on the subject? I am not good at improvising as I go along, especially in astronomical matters. But we Americans are not so easily thwarted. Quick as a wink I looked up " Equinox."

There is a renewed agitation of late to abolish Latin from our curricula. Had I not known my Latin I never could have figured out what " equinox " meant, and this article would never have been written. Take that, Mr. Flexner!

While finding " equinox," however, I came across the word " equilibrium," which is the word before you come to " equinox," and I became quite absorbed in what it had to say on the matter. There were a great many things stated there that I had never dreamed before, even in my wildest vagaries on the subject of equilibrium. For instance, did you know that if you cover the head of a bird, " as in hooding a falcon " (do you remember the good old days when you used to run away from school to hood falcons?) the bird is deprived of the power of voluntary movement? Just think of that, deprived of the power of voluntary movement simply because its head is covered!

And, as if this were not enough, it says that the same thing holds true of a fish! If you should ever, on account of a personal grudge, want to get the better of a fish, just sneak up to him on some pretext or other and suddenly cover its eyes with a cloth, and there you have it, helpless and unable to move. You may then insult it, and it can do nothing but tremble with rage.

It is little practical things like this that you pick up in reading a good reference book, things that you would never get in ten years at college.

For instance, take the word " equites," which follows " equinox " in the encyclopedia. What do you know about equites, Mr. Businessman? Of course, you remember in a vague way that they were Roman horsemen or something, but, in the broader sense of the word, could you have told that the term " equites " came, in the time of Gaius Gracchus, to mean any one who had four hundred thousand sesterces? No, I thought not. And yet that is a point which is apt to come up any day at the office. A customer from St. Paul might come in and, of course, you would take him out to lunch, hoping to land a big order. Where would you be if his hobby should happen to be " equites "? And if he should come out in the middle of the conversation with " By the way, do you remember how many sesterces it was necessary to have during the administration of Gaius Gracchus in order to belong to the Equites? " if you could snap right back at him with " Four hundred thousand, I believe," the order would be assured. And if, in addition, you could volunteer the information that an excellent account of the family life of the Equites could be found in Mommsen's "*Römisches Staatsrecht*," Vol. 3, your customer would probably not only sign up for

"If you could snap right back at him with 'Four hundred thousand, I believe,' the order would be assured."

a ten-year contract, but would insist on paying for the lunch.

But, of course, this has practically nothing to do with Spring, or, as the boys call it, the "vernal equinox." The vernal equinox is a serious matter. In fact, I think I may say without violating any confidence, that it is the initial point from which the right ascensions and the longitudes of the heavenly bodies are measured. This statement will probably bring down a storm of ridicule on my head, but look at how Fulton was ridiculed.

In fact, I might go even further and say that the way to seek out Spring is not to trail along with the poets and essayists into the woods and fields and stand about in the mud until a half-clothed bird comes out and peeps. If you really want to be in on the official advent of Spring, you may sit in a nice warm observatory and, entirely free from head-colds, proceed with the following simple course:

Take first the conception of a fictitious point which we shall call, for fun, the Mean Equinox. This Mean Equinox moves at a nearly uniform rate, slowly varying from century to century.

Now here comes the trick of the thing. The Mean Equinox is merely a decoy, and, once you have determined it, you shift suddenly to the True Equinox which you can tell, according to Professor A. M. Clerk's treatise on the subject, because it moves around the Mean Equinox in a period equal to that of the moon's nodes. Now all you have to do is to find out what the moon's nodes are (isn't it funny that you can be as familiar with an object as you are with the moon and see it almost every night, and yet never know that it has even one node, not to mention nodes?) and then find out how

HAIL, VERNAL EQUINOX!

"On the subject of spring's
arrival intuition may be led
astray."

fast they move. This done and you have discovered the Vernal Equinox, or Spring, and without
spilling a dactyl.

How much simpler this is than the old, romantic

way of determining when Spring had come! A poet
has to depend on his intuition for information, and,
on the subject of Spring's arrival, intuition may be
led astray by any number of things. You may be
sitting over one of those radiators which are con-
cealed under window-seats, for instance, and before
you are aware of it feel what you take to be the first
flush of Spring creeping over you. It would be obviously premature to go out and write a poem on
Youth and Love and Young Onions on the strength
of that.

I once heard of a young man who in November
discovered that he had an intellectual attachment
for a certain young woman and felt that married
life with her would be without doubt a success. But
he could never work himself up into sufficient emo-
tional enthusiasm to present the proposition to her
in phrases that he knew she had been accustomed to
receive from other suitors. He knew that she
wouldn't respond to a proposal of marriage couched
in terms of a real estate transaction. Yet such were
the only ones that he felt himself capable of at
the moment under the prevailing weather conditions.
So, knowing something of biology, he packed his little bag and rented an alcove in a nearby green-house,
where he basked in the intensified sun-warmth and
odor of young tube roses, until with a cry, he

smashed the glass which separated him from his
heart's desire and tore around the corner to her
house, dashing in the back door and flinging himself at her feet as she was whipping some cream,

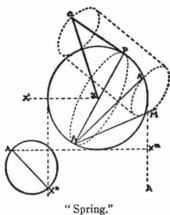

"Spring."

and there poured forth such a torrent of ardent sen-
timents that there was really nothing that the poor
girl could do but marry him that afternoon.

In fact, if you want to speak astronomically
(some people do), you may define Spring even more
definitely. Since we are all here together, and good
friends, let us take the center of the earth as origin,
and, once we have done this, the most natural fundamental axis is, obviously, the earth's rotation. The
fundamental plane perpendicular to it is the plane
of the equator. That goes without saying.

OF ALL THINGS!

Now, here we go! Coördinates referred to in this system are termed equatorial, and I think that you will agree with me that nothing could be fairer than that. Very well, then. Since this is so, we may define Spring by the following geometric representation in which the angle ZOP, made by the radius vector with the fundamental plane, shows a spring-like tendency.

This drawing we may truthfully entitle " Spring," and while it hasn't perhaps the color found in Botticelli's painting of the same name, yet it just as truthfully represents Spring in these parts as do the unstable sort of ladies in the more famous picture.

I only wish that I had more space in which to tell what my heart is full of in connection with this subject. I really have only just begun.

TABLOID EDITIONS

What I Have Made Myself Learn About You

Being An Account of How One Business Man Made the
Little Things Count. Do You?

MY business (rubber goods) was in a bad way. Somehow I couldn't seem to make it return enough to pay my income tax with. My wife and I were frankly upset.

At last one morning she came to me and said: " Fred, the baby will soon be seven months old and will have to have some sort of vocational training. What are we to do?"

That night was the bluest night I have ever spent. I thought that the end had come. Then, suddenly, the thought struck me: " Why not try character-selling? "

This may sound foolish to you. That is because it *is* foolish. But it did the trick.

I began to sell my personality. Every man that came into my store I took aside and showed him different moods. First, I would tell him a funny story, to prove to him that I was more than a mere business automaton. Then I would relate a pathetic incident I had seen on the street a week or two ago. This disclosed my heart. Then I did a fragment of a bare-foot dance and sketched a caricature of Lloyd George, to let him see that I was a man of the world. After this, I was ready to sell him what he came in for, and he would go away carrying a very definite impression of my personal characteristics—and some of my goods, in a bundle.

A week of selling rubber-goods in this manner, and I was on the vaudeville stage, earning $250 a week. How much do *you* earn?

Interesting People

A Man Who Made Good With Newts

SOME day, if you ever happen to be in Little Falls, turn to your right and you will see a prosperous-looking establishment run by Ira S. Whip, known throughout Little Falls as the newt king. Starting in with practically nothing but two congenial newts, Mr. Whip has, in the past ten years, raised no less than 4,000 of these little lizard-like animals, all of which had to be thrown away, as there is practically no market for pet newts except for incidental rôles in gold-fish tanks. But Mr. Whip did what he set out to do, and that counts for a lot in this life. Can you say as much?

The Man Who Made Good

The story of a man who made good

L ORRIE WETMORE sat disconsolately in the fountain in Madison Square Park. He was lonely. He was a failure. . . . Yes, he was. Don't contradict me. He was a terrible failure. And, as I said before, early in this story, he was lonely.

" I have fallen down on the job," he murmured to Admiral Farragut's statue. " I have not made good."

Suddenly a kind hand rested on his shoulder. He turned to face the pansy-trainer, who keeps the flower-beds in the Park in touch with the seasons.

" Don't give in, my boy," said the old man. " Remember the words of Henley, who instituted the famous Henley Regatta and so made a name for himself: ' I am the master of my Fate. I am the Captain of my Soul.' "

" By George," murmured Lorrie to the statue of Salmon P. Chase, " I *can* make good, and I *will* make good!"

And, with these words, he climbed out of the fountain and made his way resolutely across the square to the great store of Marshall Field and Co. (Advt.)

In seven weeks he was a member of the firm.

TABLOID EDITIONS

Are You Between the Ages of 7 and 94?

If so, what this eminent growth specialist says here applies
directly to you and to your family

EVERY man, woman and child between the ages
of 7 and 94 is going through a process of
growth or metamorphosis, whether they know it or
not. Are you making the most of this opportunity
which is coming to you (if your age falls within the
magic circle given above) every day of your life?
Do you realize that, during this crucial period, you
have it in your power to make what you will of yourself, provided only that you know how to go about
it and make no false steps?

As you grow from day to day, either mentally,
morally, or physically, you can say to yourself, on
awakening in the morning:

" To-day I will develop. I will grow bigger, either
mentally, morally or physically. Maybe, if it is a
nice, warm day, I will grow in all three ways at
once."

And, sure enough, when evening finds you returning home from the work of the day, it will also find
you in some way changed from the person you were
in the morning, either through the shedding of the
dry epidermis from the backs of your hands (which,
according to one of Nature's most wonderful proc-

[216]

esses, is replaced by new epidermis as soon as the old is gone), or through the addition of a fraction of an inch to your height or girth, or through some other of the inscrutable alchemies of Nature.

Think this over as you go to work, to-day, and see if it doesn't tell *you* something about *your* problem.

How I Put Myself on the Map

IT was seven o'clock at night when I first struck New York. I had come from a Middle Western town to make my fortune as a writer, and I was already discouraged. I knew no one in the Big City, and had been counting on my membership in the National Geographic Society to find me friends among my fellow-members in town. But I soon discovered that the fraternity spirit in the East was much less cordial than in my home district, and I realized, too late, that I was all alone.

With a few coins that my father had slipped into my hand as I left home, I engaged a tiny suite at the St. Regis and there set about my writing.

The first 10,000 manuscripts which I sent out, I now have. (I am at present working them over into a serial for the *Saturday Evening Post* weekly, from which I expect to make $25,000). But that is beside the point. For the purposes of the present narrative, I was a failure. The manager of the hotel was pressing me for my rent, which was already several hours overdue. I had not tipped the chamber-maid since breakfast. I sat looking out at my window, staring at the squalid wall of the Hotel Ritz. I had met New York face to face—and I had lost.

No, not lost! There was still one chance left. I sat down and, with feverish haste, wrote out a glowing account of my failure. I spared no detail of my degradation, even to taking fruit from the hotel table to my room.

Then I began to fabricate. I told how I had overcome all these handicaps and had made a success of myself. I lied. I said that I was now drawing down $200,000 a year, but that I had never forgotten my old friends. It was a good yarn, but it took me a long while to make it up. And when, at last, it was ready, I sent it to the *American Magazine.*

This is it!

How Insane Are You?

FOLLOWING is a test used in all State Hospitals to determine the fitness of the inmates for occasional shore leave. Try it on yourself and see where you get off.

Test No. 1

If you really are the reincarnation of Learning, write something here . . . but if you are being hounded by a lot of relatives whom you dislike, ring and walk in. Then, granting all this, how does it come about that you, a member of the Interstate Commerce Commission, wear no collar? . . . Ha, ha, we caught you there! But otherwise, write any letter beginning with *w* in this space. Yes, there is the space,—what's the matter with you? Go back and look again. . . . You win. Now, in spite of what the neighbors say, give three reasons for not giving three reasons why this proves that you are sane, or, as the case may be.

Through the Dobrudja with Gun and Camera

THERE was a heavy mist falling as we left Ilanlâc, rendering the *cozbars* (native *doblacs*) doubly indistinguishable. This was unfortunate, as we had planned on taking many photographs, some of which are reproduced here.

Our party consisted of seven members of the Society: Molwinch, young Houghbotham, Capt. Ramp, and myself, together with fourteen native *barbudos* (*luksni* who are under the draft age), a boat's crew, two helpers, and some potted tongue. Lieut. Furbearing, the Society's press-agent, had sailed earlier in the week, and was to join us at Curtea de Argesh.

Before us, as we progressed, lay the Tecuci, shimmering in the reflected light of the *sun* (sun). They were named by their discoverer, Joao Galatz, after his uncle, whose name was Wurgle, or, as he was known among the natives, "Wurgle." From that time (1808) until 1898, no automobile was ever seen on one of the Tecuci, although many of the inhabitants subsisted entirely on what we call " cottage-cheese."

The weevils of this district (*Curculionidæ*) are remarkable for their lack of poise. We saw several of them, just at sundown, when, according to an old native legend, the weevil comes out to defy the God of *Acor*, his ancient enemy, and never, not even in Castanheira, have I seen weevils more embarrassed than those upon whom we came suddenly at a bend in the Selch River.

Early morning found us filing up the Buzeau Valley, with the gun-bearers and bus-boys in single-file behind us, and a picturesque lot they were, too, with their lisle socks and queer patch-pockets. In taking a picture of them, I walked backward into the Buzeau River, which delayed the party, as I had, in my bag, the key with which the potted tongue cans were to be opened.

We were fortunate enough to catch several male puffins, which were so ingenuous as to eat the carpet-tacks we offered them. The puffin (*Thalassidroma buleverii*), is easily distinguishable from the more effete robin of America because the two birds are similar in no essential points. This makes it convenient for the naturalist, who might otherwise get them mixed. Puffins are hunted principally for their companionable qualities, a domesticated puffin being held the equal—if not quite—of the average Dobrudjan housewife in many respects, such as, for instance, self-respect.

It was late in the afternoon of the third day, when we finally reached Dimbovitza, and the cool *llemla* was indeed refreshing. It had been, we one and all agreed, a most interesting trip, and we vowed that we should not forget our Three Days in the Dobrudja.

Dead Leaves

" AIN'T you got them dishes done up yet, Irma? "

A petulant voice from what, in Central New England, is called the " sittin' room," penetrated the cool silence of the farm-house kitchen. Irma Hathaway passed her hand heavily before her eyes.

" Yes, Ma," she replied wearily, as she threw a cup at the steel engraving of " The Return of the Mayflower " which hung on the kitchen wall. She wondered when she would die.

A cold wind blew along the corridor which connected the kitchen with the wood-shed. Then, as if disgruntled, it blew back again, like a man returning to his room after a fresh handkerchief. Irma shuddered. It was all so inexplicably depressing.

For eighteen years the sun had never been able

to shine in Bemis Corners. God knows it had tried. But there had always been something imponderable, something monstrously bleak, which had thrown itself, like a great cloak, between the warm light of that body and the grim reality of Bemis Corners.

"If Eben had only known," thought Irma, and buried her face in the soapy water.

Some one entered the room from the wood-shed, stamping the snow from his boots. She knew, without looking up, that it was Ira.

"Why hev you come?" she said softly, lifting her moist eyes to him. It was not Ira. It was the hired man. She sobbed pitifully and leaped upon the roller-towel which hung on the door, pulling it round and round like a captive squirrel in a revolving cage.

"It ain't no use," she moaned.

And, through the cadavers of the apple-trees in the orchard behind the house, there rattled a wind from the sea, the sea to which men go down in ships never to return, telling of sorrow and all that sort of thing.

"Fate," some people call it.

To Irma Hathaway it was all the same.

TABLOID EDITIONS

TULIPS, crocuses and chard,
    And the wax bean
In the back yard.
And the open road to the land of dreams,
With the heavy swirl
Of the singing streams.
Oh! boy!

Unpublished Letters of Mark Twain

With a foreword by Albert Bigelow Paine *

FOREWORD

THIS letter from Mark Twain to Mr. Horace J. Borrow of Hartford has recently been called to my attention by a niece of Mr. Borrow's who now lives in Glastonbury. I have no reason to believe that the lady is a charlatan, in fact, I have often heard Mark Twain speak of Mr. Borrow in the highest terms.

---

* The complete works of Mark Twain, with complete forewords by Mr. Paine are, oddly enough, published by Harper and Bros. who, oddly enough, also publish this magazine. We celebrate this coincidence by offering the complete set to our readers on easy and friendly terms.

Mr. Horace J. Borrow
  Hartford, Connecticut

Dear Mr. Borrow: Enclosed find check for ten dollars ($10) in payment of my annual dues for the year 1891-2.

> Yours truly,
> (Signed) S. L. CLEMENS.

Highways and By-Ways in Old Fall River

THE chance visitor to Fall River may be said, like the old fisherman in " Bartholomew Fair," to have " seen half the world, without tasting its savor." Wandering down the Main Street, with its clanging trolley-cars and noisy drays, one wonders (as, indeed, one may well wonder), if all this is a manifestation so much of Fall River as it is of that for which Fall River stands.

Frankly, I do not know.

But there is something in the air, something in-effable in the swirl of the smoke from the towering stacks, which sings, to the rhythm of the clashing shuttles and humming looms, of a day when old gentlemen in belted raglans and cloth-topped boots strolled through these streets, bearing with them the legend of mutability. Perhaps " mutability " is too strong a word. Fall Riverians would think so.

TABLOID EDITIONS

And the old Fall River Line! What memories does that name not awaken in the minds of globe-trotters? Or, rather, what memories *does* it awaken? William Lloyd Garrison is said to have remarked upon one occasion to Benjamin Butler that one of the most grateful features of Fall River was the night-boat for New York. To which Butler is reported to have replied: "But, my dear Lloyd, there is no night-boat to New York, and there won't be until along about 1875 or even later. So your funny crack, in its essential detail, falls flat."

But, regardless of all this, the fact remains that Fall River is Fall River, and that it is within easy motoring distance of Newport, which offers our art department countless opportunities for charming illustrations.

The Editor's Drawer

LITTLE Bobby, aged five, saying his prayers, had come to that most critical of diplomatic crises: the naming of relatives to be blessed.

"Why don't I ask God to bless Aunt Mabel?" he queried, looking up with a roguish twinkle in his blue eyes.

"But you do, Bobby," answered his mother.

"So I do," was his prompt reply.

LITTLE Willy, aged seven, was asked by his teacher to define the word " confuse."

" ' Confuse ' is what my daddy says when he looks at his watch," said Willy. The teacher never asked that question again. At least, not of Willy.

LITTLE Gertrude, aged three, was saying her prayers. " Is God everywhere? " she asked.

" Yes, dear, everywhere," answered her mother.

" *Everywhere?* " she persisted.

" Yes, dear, *everywhere,*" repeated her mother, all unsuspecting.

" Then He must be like Uncle Ned," said the little tot.

" Why, Gertrude, what makes you say that? "

" Because I heard Daddy say that Uncle Ned was everywhere," was the astounding reply.

THE LAST MATCH

By Roy Comfort Ashurst

SLOWLY the girl in the green hat approached the swinging door of the hotel.

She was thinking.

A man more versed in the ways of womankind than Ned Pillsbury might, perhaps, have perceived that she was also glancing surreptitiously upwards through the dark fringe of lashes which veiled her brown gypsy eyes, but Ned was not a trained observer in such matters. To him, as he sat in the large, roomy leather chair in the lobby, the only reaction was

(*Continued on page 49*)

ARE YOU SURE OF YOUR CRANK-SHAFT?

The answer to this question is the answer to the peace of mind with which you operate your motor. Whether you are the operator of an automobile, or one of those intrepid spirits to whom the world-war has given the vision of flying through the air at

[228]

175 miles an hour, you need to give pause and say to yourself:

"Just how much faith can I put in my crank-shaft?"

And if it is a Zimco crank-shaft, made in the factory of a thousand sky-lights, you may be sure that it will stand the test.

Zimco crank-shafts have that indefinable quality which gives them personality among crank-shafts. You know a Zimco when you see one and you feel that it is an old friend. It does everything but speak. And that its host of friends do for it.

Let us send you free our handsome little booklet on "After-the-War-Problems."

(Continued from page 8)
one of amazement that there could be such a beautiful person alive in this generation.

Ned was a young man of great possibilities, but few probabilities. Born in the confusion of an up-state city, and educated in the hub-bub of a large college, on whose foot-ball team he had distinguished himself in the position of left-half-back, he had never been so fortunate as to receive that quiet instruction in dark brown eyelashes and their potentialities which has been found to be so highly essential to the equipment
(Continued on page 107)

INTRODUCING THE 7-TON GARGANTUA TRUCK

This important announcement is made by the Gargantua Company with a full realization of its significance. We realize that we are creating a new thing in trucks.

The Gargantua combines all the qualities of the truck with the conveniences of a Fall River boat. Its transmission system has been called "The Queen of Transmissions." The efficacy of its bull-pinions in the tractor attachment has been the subject of enthusiastic praise from bull-pinion experts on all continents.

The Gargantua is the result of a dream. Henry L. McFern (now president of the Gargantua Co.), was the dreamer. Mr. McFern wanted something that would revolutionize the truck business, and yet still be a truck. He gave it the thought of all his waking hours. His friends called him a " dreamer," but Henry McFern only smiled. When first he brought out the model of the Gargantua it was called " McFern's Folly," but Henry McFern only smiled the more. And when the time came for the test, it was seen that the " dreamer " of South Bend had given the world a *new* Idea.

(Continued from page 49)

of a man of the world to-day. He knew that women were strange creatures, for this popular superstition reaches even to the recesses of the most exclusive of male retreats, but further than that he was uninformed. He had, it is true, like many another young man, felt the influence of certain pairs of blue eyes

(Continued on page 113)

I AM THE STRENGTH OF AGES

¶ I have sprung from the depths of the hills.

¶ Before the rivers were brought forth, or even before the green leaves in their softness made the landscape, I was your servant.

¶ From the bowels of the earth, where men toil in darknesss, I come, bringing a message of insuperable strength.

¶ From sun to sun I meet and overcome the forces of nature, brothers of mine, yet opponents; kindred, yet foes.

¶ I am silent, but my voice re-echoes beyond the ends of the earth.

¶ I am master, yet I am slave.

¶ I am Woonsocket Wrought Iron Pipe, "the Strongest in the Long Run." (Trademark.)

Send for illustrated booklet entitled

"The Romance of Iron Pipe."

(*Continued from page 107*)
which had come into his life during the years when he was in susceptible moods, but such occurrences were not the result of any realization on his part of their significance. They were in the same category of physical phenomena as includes measles or chicken-pox, for example,—the direct result of a certain
(*Continued on page 125*)

TABLOID EDITIONS

WHY WORRY OVER CHISEL TROUBLES?

" You've got the right kind of chisel there. I see
it's a Blimco. I've always found that Blimco chisels
stand up longer under everyday usage, and I tell my
foremen to see to it that the men always have their
Blimcoes and no other. I have tried the others, but
have always come back to the Blimco. I suppose it
is because the Blimco is made by master-workmen,
supervised by experts and sold only by dealers who
know the best tools. When you see a Blimco in a
dealer's window, you may know that that dealer is a
man of discrimination. The discriminating workman
always uses a Blimco. ' The Chisel of Distinction.'
Clip this coupon and send it NOW for our instructive
booklet ' Chiselling Prosperity '."

(Continued from page 113)
temporary debility which renders the patient susceptible to
infection.

Ned Pillsbury was therefore somewhat overcome by the
vision of the girl with the green hat, and suffered from that
feeling of pioneering emotion which must have affected Mr.
Balboa who, according to the poet, stood "silent on a peak in
Darien" survey-

(Continued on page 140)

MAKE YOUR PISTON-RINGS WORK FOR YOU

Why should you persist in being ashamed of your
piston-rings?

[232]

Why should you make your wife and daughter suffer the humiliation which comes from knowing that you are using an inferior make?

" Emancipator " Piston-Rings cost more than ordinary piston-rings, but they are worth it. They are worth more even than we ask.

What would it mean to you to know that you were not losing steam power because of a faulty piston-ring? Wouldn't it be worth a few extra dollars?

Napoleon once said that an army marches on its stomach.

If this has any relation to piston-rings, we fail to see it. But it has as much relation to piston-rings as a matter of price does when steam economy is at stake.

" Emancipator " Piston-Rings bring twice the power with one-half the trouble. That's why we call them " Emancipator."

Ask your grocer about " Emancipators." He will tell you to ask your garage-man. In the meantime, let us send you our catalog.

(*Continued from page 125*)
ing the Pacific. He was aware of a strange exaltation coursing through his veins, and before he knew it, he was on his feet and pushing through the revolving door in the compartment behind the green hat.
(*Continued on page 156*)

TABLOID EDITIONS

YOU, MR. LEATHER-BELTING-USER!

What is your problem?

Do you wake up in the morning with green spots before your eyes? Are you depressed? Does the thought of a day's work with an unsatisfactory belting weigh upon your mind, bringing on acidosis, hardening of the arteries, and a feeling of opposition to the League of Nations?

If so, let us tackle your problem for you.

We have built up a service department which stands alone in its field. For sixteen years we have been making it the perfect institution that it is to-day.

Bring your belting troubles to Mr. Henry W. Wurlitz, who is at the head of our service department, and he will set you right. He will show you the way to a Bigger, Better, Belting outlook.

(Continued from page 140)
"I beg your pardon," he said softly, as they emerged on the street, "but did you drop this flask?"
She turned quickly and faced him. There was a twinkle in her dark brown eyes as she answered him:
(To be continued)